THE UNEXPECTED

Can an unexpected letter change your life?

The Unexpected Letter
Book 2 in the Unexpected series

DL GALLIE

Published by DL Gallie Author

First published 30th May 2019 in the Calendar Gals series as 'December'

Second Edition, 10th November 2019

Edited by Karen Hrdlicka, Barren Acres Editing

Cover Design by Dana Leah of Designs by Dana

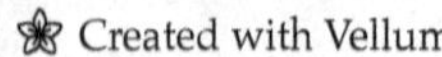 Created with Vellum

Could an unexpected letter change your life?

When it rains, it pours for me.
I discover I'm pregnant, with my dead fiancé's baby, on
the same day I'm due to bury him.

In my time of despair and need, I turn to Branson, my
dead fiancé's brother, best friend, and business partner. He
doesn't hesitate to offer me unwavering support at this
difficult time; it's the least he can do for his brother and
the mother of his niece or nephew.

When I begin to develop feelings for him, I put it down to
pregnancy hormones, but an unexpected letter changes
everything.

THE UNEXPECTED SERIES

The Unexpected Gift

The Unexpected Letter

The Unexpected Package

The Unexpected Connection

ALSO BY DL GALLIE

THE CASTAWAY GROVE COLLECTION

Love has arrived in the Grove

Oasis

Unequivocal Love

Five Words

Broken Rules - coming mid / late 2020

…and a few more as well.

THE LIQUOR CABINET SERIES

Liquor has never been so disturbingly saucy

Malt Me (Book 1)

Tequila Healing (Book 2)

Wine Not (Book 3)

The Final Shot (Book 4)

The Liquor Cabinet: Series boxset

STAND ALONES

Out of Nowhere

Antecedent

Seven Nights

Falling for Dr. Kelly, a Falling novel

Falling for Dr. Knight, a Falling novel - coming May 2020

Doc Steel - coming June 2020

The Dirty Dozen: Alpha edition

The Rule Breaker Anthology - coming soon

In the Dark of Night anthology (only available in paperback directly from me)

Titanic Tales, a charity anthology (no longer available)

Gone Coastal, a sizzling summer beach anthology (no longer available)

Leave Me Breathless: The Lilac Collection (no longer available)

A NOTE FROM THE AUTHOR

This book was originally published in May 2019 as December, book 12 in the Calendar Gals series.

It is the same story with a new title, this version has an extended epilogue giving you a peek into Kasey and Branson's life after the original epilogue.

To all those who have loved and lost,
and found love again

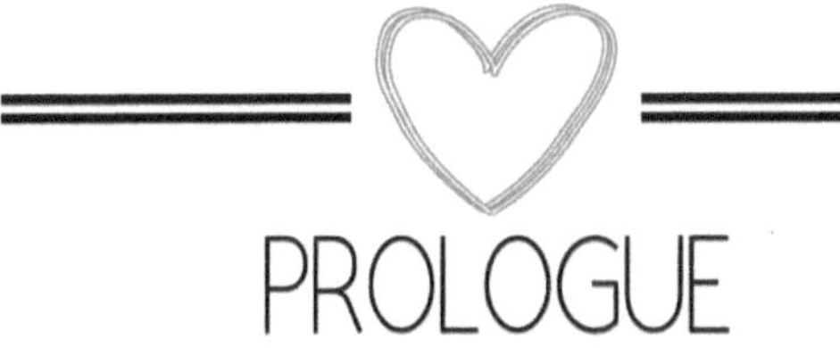

PROLOGUE

THERE WAS A POINT IN TIME WHEN I THOUGHT MY LIFE WAS over. The hits kept coming but there was always a constant in my life. That constant kept me going but it could never be more.

One day, I found a letter and everything shifted. Something I didn't know I needed was unleashed and life had meaning once again. Who knew one letter had the power to change the course of my life? He did, and that's why he left it.

This is the story of my unexpected letter.

CHAPTER 1

… May 5th, 2019

MY GIRLFRIENDS HAVE SURPRISED ME WITH A BACHELORETTE weekend away…to Kansas, of all places, but Stacey assures me that it's 'totally worth the trip.' I'm yet to see that, or anything, because I'm currently blindfolded, sitting in the back of a stretch Hummer.

The bubbly is flowing. The laughs are a plenty and the atmosphere is electric, and everyone is having fun; blindfolded me included.

The car stops and a few moments later the driver opens the door. "Ladies, you have arrived," he says, as he takes my hand and helps me out. It's really disorientating being blindfolded but at the same time it's exhilarating and exciting. It reminds me of my birthday last year...

...February 27th, 2018

"Branson, where are you taking me and WHY the friggin' hell am I blindfolded?"

"Because!" he playfully replies.

"Because? Really? That's all I get?"

"Yep. Now get in, and watch your head. If you turn up injured, Kody will kick my ass."

"I'll kick your ass for not telling me where we are going."

"I'd like to see you try." He pauses and I can tell he's grinning right now. "Now get in."

"You're a bossy boots," I huff.

"Says the queen of bossy."

"I'm not bossy," I scoff, whacking the air—hoping to get Branson—but instead my knuckles hit the car door. "Shit!" I shout, shaking my hand to ease the pain.

Suddenly, my hand is enveloped in warmth and I feel soft lips pressed against my knuckles. "There all better," Branson huskily whispers.

"My hero," I singsong.

"If it wasn't your birthday, I'd totally smack your ass for being cheeky."

"Maybe I want to be smacked," I mischievously reply.

It's suddenly silent, the only sound to be heard is each of us breathing. It's awkward but not, the moment is broken when Branson taps my side. "Come on, we better get going, otherwise you'll be late."

"Late for what?" I question.

"Wouldn't you like to know?"

"Umm, yes, that's why I asked."

"Shut up and get in, birthday brat."

Just like that, Branson and I are back to our usual playful selves. With a smile, I carefully climb in and await my surprise. We don't drive for long and when we arrive, Branson tells me to wait there—like I'm going to go anywhere on my own blindfolded. The car door opens and Branson carefully escorts me out of the vehicle, down a walkway, through several doors, and then we stop. Branson lifts my blindfold off and I'm met with a chorus of "Surprise" and "Happy Birthday," deafening cheers and claps.

My eyes lock on Kody's and I smile. He saunters over to me, wrapping his arms around my waist. "Happy birthday, gorgeous!" he says, before he plants a searing hot kiss on my lips.

Pulling back, I grip both his hands and squeeze. "Thanks for this, babe, it was totally unexpected."

"Don't thank me, thank him." He points to Branson, who is smiling sheepishly from behind us.

Stepping over to Branson, I kiss him on the cheek and hug him, "Thank you Branson."

He hugs me back and quietly murmurs, "Your welcome, Kase. I'd do anything to see you happy. Happy birthday."

He steps back and walks over to his parents, just as Kody wraps his arms around me from behind. He nuzzles my neck and whispers, "Make sure you keep that blindfold, I'm getting all sorts of kinky sexy ideas for later."

Spinning around, I give him a wink. "You had me at kinky." I kiss his jaw, blissfully happy at my surprise party and totally in love with Kody Holmes...

Remembering that night, I squeeze my thighs together and decide I'm TOTALLY keeping this blindfold for when I get home, Kody and I are going to have some blindfolded fun…again.

"What are you grinning about?" Stacey asks me.

"Nothing, I'm just really excited for the night ahead."

"Mmmhmpf." I know that tone from her, she doesn't believe me at all, but thankfully she doesn't push me. With a sigh, I stand on the pavement, blindfolded, and wait while the girls all climb out. Suddenly, there are hands on my shoulders, and Stacey says from behind me, "Let's go." She pushes me forward. "Okay, babe, there are," she pauses for a bit, "seven steps and then the fun is going to begin."

Somehow, I make it up the stairs without tripping, or breaking anything. I'm grinning when a deep husky voice says, "Welcome, ladies. My name is Marcus, let me know if I can be of any assistance this evening."

"You can tell me where I am?" I ask.

He takes my hand and kisses the back of it. "Nice try, Kasey. Just go with the flow and enjoy yourself." With my sight gone, his voice is prominent and ohh so fine…*I bet he's butt-ugly,* I think to myself and giggle as I'm pushed farther into the establishment.

"You know my name?" I ask, but I'm met with silence.

We stop walking again and Stacey says, "Well, der, of course, you are the main star tonight," I swear she silently adds, "except for those up on stage." This piques my curiosity.

"Oooookay," I offer in reply.

Stacey is now quietly talking to someone and I'm left alone, blindfolded in the middle of, I don't know where in Kanas. I shake my head and again giggle to myself.

"Let's go," Stacey suddenly says, a door opens, and we walk inside. There's music thumping. Women are chattering and giggling. Glasses are clinking and I'm now guessing we are in a bar. We stop suddenly and Stace lifts off my blindfold. Blinking a few times, my vision comes back, and I look to Stacey, she's grinning from ear to ear and raises her eyebrows seductively at me before she excitedly screams, "Welcome to Bare Chested!"

"Huh?" I ask confused.

"We will be seeing our very own sexy schmexy strip show…right after Marcus here," she flicks her eyes to the left where I see a sexy as sin guy hungrily staring and walking toward me, "gives you an up close and personal lap dance."

My mouth drops open in shock. I remember mentioning to Stace that I have always wanted to go to a strip club, but I never expected this. "Stacey," I say, my eyes well with tears.

"Nope, no crying." She shakes her head. "Now, sit back and enjoy." She pushes my shoulders and I drop down on to the seat. My phone rings and it's Branson's tone. "Nope, he can wait," Stacey says, as she hands me another shot, I throw it back and shrug, after all, who am I to argue when a sexy guy is prowling toward me.

"WooooHooooo," I shout, as he saunters over to me.

A glass of bubbly is thrust into my hand; I drink the entire thing and slam the empty glass onto the table next to me. Marcus is now in front of me, grinding his hips in circles. "This is so hot," I giggle as he rests his hands on the couch arms, cocooning me.

"Hey."

"Hey," I giggle in reply, yes, I giggle like a schoolgirl. Suddenly the bubbly from the limo and the shot I just skulled hit me with force. My phone rings again, but before I can say anything, Stacey digs it out and silences it.

Marcus grabs my chin and turns my attention back to him. He sexily spins about and now has his back to me, shaking his tight sexy ass in my face. Leaning forward, I mimic licking when he reaches behind him, grabs my hands and pulls me forward. My face is pressed against his back and he runs my hands up and down his abs. Holy muscles, Batman, I throw my head back and laugh. The girls all laugh and smile. This is so fun and so sexy at the same time, *I wonder if I can persuade Kody to do something like this for me when I get home?*

All too soon, my dance is over. Marcus lifts my hand and places a kiss on the back, just like when we arrived. "You will make a beautiful bride," he says, before turning and sauntering away.

Another glass of bubbly appears, and I drink it slowly. I look around; everyone is smiling, laughing, and having the best time. "Stacey, this is awesome and the best night ever." I pause and swallow the lump in my throat. "Thanks so much."

The lights on the stage dim and she leans into me and whispers, "The fun is just starting, babe."

A song I don't recognize begins to play and the sexiest guy ever struts his stuff on stage in nothing but black pants and a tie…and he wears the hell out of that tie. I scream and holler like the others in the club. He introduces himself as Jake and then he's asking about a bachelorette party and starts walking down the stage stairs. He comes over to us, his eyes are locked on Karen, her face turns beet red. "Are you the lucky lady whose getting married?" His voice is deep and ohh so sexy.

Karen turns to me, grabs my wrist, and shouts, "No, but she is," as she shoves me toward him.

"Well, aren't you a beautiful woman?" he croons. "Your

soon-to-be husband is a lucky man." He takes my hand, pulls out a chair, and gently pushes me down to take a seat. He spins around and shakes his ass in my face, once again I giggle and laugh. Someone yells for me to squeeze his butt, I'd really like to, but I'm not sure of the protocol in a club like this, so I keep my hands in my lap. But my eyes travel all over this body. There isn't an ounce of fat on him, and he has muscles that I have never seen up close before.

He spins back to face me and grabs my hands, running them up and down his abs...his rock-hard abs. My eyes land on his and he winks at me, just as I hear Stacey yelling my name. Turing to face her, I see tears welling in her eyes. She holds the phone to my ear. "Hello," I breathlessly say into the phone.

"Kace, it's Branson." Instantly, my body freezes, his tone is off.

"What's wrong?" I ask, I hold my breath and wait for his reply. Without him saying anything, I know it's bad news.

"Kody..."

"No, no, no." I say into the phone, shoving Jake away with all my might, he stumbles backward as I stand up. "...he didn't make it." I'm frozen on the spot, I shake my head from side to side as tears cascade down my cheeks; everything around me fades out. Branson is talking but I don't hear anything. In my head, over and over I just keep repeating the last thing I clearly heard Branson say to me 'he didn't make it.'

A guttural scream passes my lips. Falling to my knees, I drop the phone and collapse into a heap. Everything around me goes silent; Stacey squats down and rubs my back. I can feel everyone's gaze on me but I feel so alone right in this moment. My heart is shattering into a million fragments. My life will be altered from this moment forward. From next to me I hear Stacey say over and over, "Shit, shit, shit."

She wraps her arms around me and pulls me into her chest as the world around me crumbles. "Kasey, babe. I'm so sorry."

"What's going on?" Karen asks.

Looking up at her, I don't know what to say. My heads starts shaking from side to side again and I cover my mouth, as a fresh batch of tears fall.

Stacey looks over at her and sadly says, "It's Kody. He's dead."

CHAPTER 2

… May 12th, 2019

Sitting on the edge of the bath, I hold the stick in my shaking hands and look down. My eyes well with tears as I stare at the two pink lines in the little window. Those two pink lines are staring back up at me, laughing their pink little asses off.

How much more shit can be thrown at me?

Shaking my head, I throw the stick on the counter, lean my elbows on my knees, and lower my head. Sadness mixed with happiness mixed with complete and utter devastation envelops me. Kody and I had wanted this for so long, and just my luck—when it finally happens—he's not here to enjoy it with me. He would have been the bestest dad. Sitting up straight, I rest my palm on my belly and shake my head.

The tears start to fall…again, what an ironic fucking twist of fate this is. *Fuck you, Alanis Morrissette and your stupid song.* Breaking the silence is a knock at the bathroom door. "Kasey, you all right in there?" Stacey asks me.

"Yeah," I sniff. "Be right out."

Stacey has been with me twenty-four seven since I received the call about Kody. Without her, I don't know how I would have coped, or returned to Chicago. Without her, I'd still be stuck in Kansas. After that fateful phone call from Branson, she went into savior mode and got me home as quick as she could.

Standing up, I pick up the stick and tuck it into my dress pocket. Lifting my head, I stare at my reflection in the mirror; I don't recognize the person staring back at me. My eyes are puffy, red, and bloodshot. I have massive black bags under my lashes. I look and feel like shit too, but I guess now I know why…I'm fucking pregnant. The real kick in the guts is that at a time when I'm meant to be over the moon happy, I'm lower than low. In an hour's time, I'll be saying goodbye to my fiancé. My best friend. My baby daddy.

Is he still my fiancé if he's dead?

Opening the bathroom door, I yell, "Hey, Stace, is he still my fiancé if he's dead?"

She stares at me blankly. "Ummm, I don't know."

"What don't you know?" Branson asks as he walks into my and Kody's, well *my*, bedroom.

"Is Kody still my fiancé if he's dead?" I ask.

"Ummm." He stops midstep, "I, umm, ahhh—"

"Wow, great help there, guys," I snap out of frustration that no one knows the answer to my completely random question. "I thought you knew everything, Branson," I retort in a bitchy tone.

"Kase, I don't think you need to worry about that right now," Branson says. "It's time to go." I stare at him, frozen on the spot.

My head starts shaking from side to side. "I...I can't do this," I whine, "How do I say good bye to my fiancé and ba—" I cut myself off; I don't want to share this news with anyone just yet. "Branson, please don't make me do this. Please tell me this is a horrible dream, and I'm going to wake up, and when I walk downstairs I'll find Kody playing that dumb fucking game on his phone." I pause, looking up at him with tears pouring down my cheeks. I plead, "Please tell me this isn't real. Please, Branson. Please." Falling to my knees, I break down...for the millionth time in the last seven days. My body shudders as grief overtakes me. My sobs and cries mix into a horrendous howl.

Branson races over to me and wraps his arms around me. "Shhhh, it's going to me all right, Kase. We will get through this together," he whispers, running his hand soothingly up and down my back.

"I miss him sooo much, Branson," I blubber. "And now, I don't know what to do. I can't say goodbye because then it all becomes real."

"Kace, you will get through this. You are the strongest person I know."

Staring at him though my tears, I sadly smile at him, calling bullshit on what he just said. As I stare at him, I realize I'll now need him more than ever. Branson is my rock, my crying partner, my everything. Out of everyone, he feels the loss of Kody just as much as I do, but in a different way. He lost his brother, best friend, and business partner. In the last few days, I've found myself leaning on him in a way I didn't think possible. However, with what I'm currently hiding in my pocket, and with his niece or nephew growing in my belly—over the next nine months —I'm going to need him more than I have ever needed anyone before.

CHAPTER 3

Once I've composed myself, Branson and Stacey escort me down the hall. Entering the living room, I stop as I take in everyone who is here. Kody and Branson's parents, Randall and Helen Holmes are on the couch. My parents, Trudy and Steve Wellson are sitting at the dining table, and Gage and Marlee from work are by the fireplace.

They all look up and sadly smile at me. *I hate sad smiles. I hate everything at the moment.* As I walk farther in to the room, the air around me fills with sadness, grief, and unhappiness. My eyes lock on Mom's and once again they fill with tears. Her mom instinct kicks in and she quickly walks over to me, wrapping her arms around me tightly; just like she did when I was little and upset. Dad joins us and the three of us hug in the middle of the room, my wails becoming louder and louder. "Ohh, baby," Mom says, as she grips my cheeks and sadly smiles at me.

"I'm okay, Mom. Well, I think I am. Actually, I have no fucking clue how I feel right at this moment." She raises her eyes at me about my language. "Sorry, Mom, I won't swear again."

"I'll let it pass, just this once, but don't make a habit of it."

With that one sentence, my mouth slightly lifts into a grin. "Remember the first time you met Kody? He was so nervous that every second word out of his mouth was a cuss."

"He did not?" Helen asks, her voice laced with shock.

Nodding my head, I laugh as Mom sits next to Helen. "He sure did," Mom says.

Shaking my head, I remember the day clearly...

..."What if they hate me?" Kody asks as we drive over to my parents' house for dinner.

"Babe, they will love you. Just like I do."

"Say it again."

"I love you, Kody Holmes, with all my heart and soul."

"I love you too, Kasey Wellson."

Pulling my car into the driveway of my childhood home, I smile. The house looks just the same as it did when I grew up, just with no toys scattered across the front lawn, or bike leaning against the house. Dad's rose garden at the front is still blooming; it's his pride and joy.

"Wow, your mom has as amazing rose garden," Kody says as I turn off the car and we climb out.

"Actually, it's Dad's baby."

"No fucking way?" he says, as he laces his fingers with mine and we walk up the path.

"Yes, way," Mom says, her tone not impressed.

"Fuck," Kody mumbles, loud enough for Mom to hear.

"Shit, fuck, umm, ahhh, Mrs. Wellson. I'm Kody Holmes." He drops my hand and outstretches his hand to Mom.

"Call me, Trudy," she says, taking his hand in hers and shaking.

"Pumpkin," Dad says from the front steps.

"Daddy," I reply, stepping toward him. He envelops me in a hug and whispers, "He's off to a colorful start." I giggle into his shoulder and tug him toward Kody.

"Dad, this is Kody. Kody, this is my dad, Steve."

"Mr. Wellson, it's lovely to meet you."

"Steve," Dad sternly says, outstretching his hand to Kody. They shake and Kody nods.

"Steve, you have a fucking beautiful garden." He pauses and his eyes bug open, Mom's mouth drops in shock.

"Fuck!" he loudly mumbles. Dad and I laugh. "Oh My God, Mrs. Kasey, I mean Mrs. Wellson, shit, Trudy, I'm so fucking sorry. I don't fucking know, shit, what the hell has come over me."

Dad and I are now laughing our asses off. Mom isn't impressed, and Kody is mortified. It will go down as the best parent introduction ever...

After my trip down memory lane, I giggle and add, "The next time I spoke to Mom, she told me a man who swears like that would never be good enough for me. Kody proved her wrong. He never swore in front of her again, and he proved that he..." I swallow the lump in my throat, "he was the best man ever."

The room goes quiet as we all silently reminisce and remember Kody. My happy memories are interrupted when I hear two fateful words. "It's time," Branson says, as he steps over to me. Staring blankly at him, I nod my head and take a deep breath. My body goes into autopilot and I follow everyone out to the cars.

Before I know it, we arrive at the funeral home. We all climb out of the cars and silently walk inside. The room goes silent when I enter, I somberly walk between the pews toward the front, my grip on Branson's arm getting tighter and tighter with each step I take. My eyes are locked on the casket at the front; it's adorned with his *Red Sox* and *Blackhawks* jerseys, and a beautiful floral arrangement. *Kody would love this*, I think to myself as I take my seat in the front row.

The funeral passes me by in a blur; the only thing I really remember is when Branson left my side to give the eulogy. When he stepped away from me, I felt lost and abandoned, even though I was in a room with hundreds of other people. Without him by my side, I felt alone and bereft. My mind started to drift into the darkness...until I heard him speak. His voice drew me back into the present and as I listened to him talk about Kody, a sense of calm and peace washed over me. This feeling has been absent since I received that call.

"Kody was my big brother. My business partner and my best friend. I don't know how I will go on without seeing his stupid face every day. He was the best person I know, and the world will be empty without him in it.

There were many wonderful aspects to Kody's life, and he touched our lives in a way like no other. He will be remembered as a wonderful brother, a great friend, a generous person, and a loving fiancé to Kasey. Kasey brought him to life when they met, and I don't think I'd ever seen him as happy as he was with her. He died a happy man and it was all due to her.

"Kody made our lives richer and fuller. Now that he has passed away, of course there is emptiness, pain, and confusion, and maybe even anger at death coming to a man of only thirty-three. However, in many ways, the gift of his life is still here with us, especially in our hearts. He lives on in our memories and stories. I encourage you to share—today, tomorrow, and in the years to come—your memories and stories. In this way we will keep the gift of Kody's life alive.

"On behalf of Mom, Dad, Kasey, and me, I'd like to thank you all for coming here today. Please join us at Bin 501 to celebrate the life of my brother, Kody Randall Holmes."

Next thing I know, I'm sitting in Bin 501. Everyone around me is reminiscing about Kody and how wonderful he was. Was, I fucking hate that word right now. A glass of wine is placed in my hand. Lifting it to my lips, I take a sip and then I remember. Quickly, I stand up, slamming the glass down on the table and race outside.

Leaning against the brick building, I close eyes and look to the sky. "Why Kody, why? Why did you leave me?" I ask the universe.

"Kase, are you okay?" Gage asks me, his face etched with worry. It's nice to see worry and not sympathy staring back at me.

"Gage, I..." I don't finish my sentence; I burst into tears once again. Gage steps toward me and wraps his arms around my waist. Burrowing my head into his shoulder, I let it all out. I let out everything I withheld during the funeral, I didn't want to be the 'the fiancé who fell apart at the funeral.' Opening my eyes, I see Marlee beside us and my eyes gravitate to her hand resting lovingly on Gage and my knees buckle. Falling to the pavement, I completely shatter. The grief and emotion of the day catch up to me, and I disintegrate into a sobbing mess as Gage drops down next to me and rubs my back.

Suddenly I'm pulled into someone's arms and I know I'm now in Branson's embrace. He holds me tight and whispers, "Shhhh, let it all out. I've got you."

His words cause me to fall apart further. These are the exact words Kody whispered to me on the day I got my last period, when I broke down in our en suite at seeing my underwear tinged pink. Then it hits me again: I'm pregnant and I just buried my fiancé and baby daddy. "Branson, I can't do this. I can't do this alone."

He pulls back from me, grips my shoulders and says, "Kase, I'm here. You will get through this. Once the grief passes, life will go on. Kody would want you to live life to the fullest. Now you need to live for two."

"Three," I whisper.

"Huh?" he questions me.

"I'm pregnant, Branson."

CHAPTER 4

shock.

Nodding my head, I confirm, "Yep, inside my belly right now is your niece or nephew. One last parting gift from Kody." Looking up at Branson, I cry, "How can I have a baby alone? How will I do this when I can barely get out of bed now? How am I going to survive? I can't do this without him. I just can't." Tears cascade down my cheeks. My chest heaves as the grief and emotions of the day and my morning discovery catch up to me.

Falling into Branson's chest, I let it all out. He once again holds me tight. "Shhhh, let it all out. I've got you." His embrace is comforting and just what I need.

The last tear has fallen, and I'm completely wiped out,

I look up at Branson and smile, "Thank you, Branson. I don't know what I would do without you."

"You'll never find out."

"I'll hold you to that."

"Kase, I will be here every step of the way. My niece or nephew is going to be loved doubly from me, and they will know how awesome and amazing their daddy was."

This causes me to tear up again. "Branson, I'm going to be a single mom. I won't have Kody to watch and learn from. What if I'm shit at it?"

"Kasey, you'll be fine. You are strong and resilient. You will rock as a mom." He pauses. "You've got this, and me too. I'll be here every step of the way."

"I can't ask you to do that. You have a life. A business."

"I can multi-task." That causes me to laugh. "Okay, we both know I can't, but I can learn. I'm here no matter what, Kase. Kody would kick my ass if I left you to do this by yourself."

"Yeah, I'd like to see that. He wouldn't hurt a fly, let alone you."

"That's true. He had a heart of gold. Man, I'm going to miss him."

"You and me both." Taking a deep breath, I swallow deeply, before I reach out and squeeze his hand. "Thank you, Branson. Thank you for everything now and in the future."

"Happy to help. Now let's get back inside and celebrate your good news."

Shaking my head, I shout, "No! Not yet. I don't want to tell anyone until it's safe. I can't handle any more sympathy."

"Fair enough, let's go back in and celebrate Kody and share embarrassing stories about him."

With a smile I nod. "I'd like that."

Linking my arm through Branson's, we head back inside. As soon as I step in, Mom races over to me. "You okay, baby?"

Nodding, I sadly smile. "Yeah, I'm okay, Mom. It's just tough, but Branson made me realize Kody wouldn't want me to dwell on his passing. He'd want me to be happy and that's what I'm going to do…" Turning to face the room, I shout, "Can I have your attention please?" The room goes quiet and all eyes are on me. "First of all, I want to thank everyone for coming today. Kody would be amazed with the turn out. H—"

"Who knew he had so many friends?" someone in the back shouts, garnering a laugh from everyone.

"He will be missed by many but he will live on in all of us." My eyes drop to my belly and I smile, knowing that a part of him is still here with me. A part of him is growing inside of me. "The time for mourning has passed, it's time to live and celebrate Kody. He and Branson opened this bar together, his legacy will live on here…and in many other ways. Kody," I tear up and swallow deeply, "Kody, I love you with all my heart and soul. I'll miss you every day for the rest…" I pause and swallow the emotion building, when from behind me, a hand squeezes my shoulder, Branson whispers, "You've got this."

Looking back over my shoulder, I smile. Taking a deep breath, I continue, "Every day I will miss you. I'll try to move on and be happy but when you were taken, a part of me was too. I'll never be the same, but I will do my best to live for the both of us."

"Here, here!" Randall shouts. Everyone cheers and salutes Kody. Randall walks over to me and takes my hand in his; he squeezes it tightly and stares at me. "Kody loved you just as much as I love Helen. You will always be part of this family, even if it's not official."

"Thanks, Mr. H." Wrapping my arms around him, I give him a hug. "I'd really like that." It's on the tip of my tongue to tell him I'm pregnant, but I don't want to tell anyone, in case I lose it. Helen walks over and pulls me from his grasp, when we hug, it's a mommy hug and I begin to cry again. "I miss him too," she whispers. "No parent should bury their child, I just can't believe he's gone."

"You and me both," I say as I pull back, "I keep hoping it's a terrible nightmare and that I'll wake up and see him smiling back at me. Or hear him singing off-key in another room."

"Ohh, he was a horrible singer," she laughs.

"The worst," I giggle.

Glancing around the bar, I see how many people loved Kody. The atmosphere is a mixture of sadness and laughter, as everyone remembers their time with Kody. Resting my hand on my belly, I smile. I know that Peanut and I will have the love and support of our friends, his and my family, and everything will be okay. My eyes gravitate toward Branson chatting with Gage and Marlee; I find myself smiling, genuinely smiling. He must sense my gaze upon him because he looks over to me and grins back. Branson is my rock, my everything at the moment, and I'm lucky to have him by my side and in our life.

As I stand here talking with his mom and dad, I know Peanut and I will be just fine.

CHAPTER 5

…June 26th, 2019

"You are glowing," Branson says, as he places the grocery bag on the counter. Hopping up from the sofa, I walk over and take a seat at the breakfast bar, and he hands me the jar of salsa and another bag of snow peas. Thirty minutes ago I called him in a fluster that I had run out and I was in dire need of them. He made a special trip to Jewell-Osco, at 10:00 p.m. to grab them for me and drop them over. Spicy salsa and snow peas are my life. I eat them for breakfast, lunch, dinner, and snack on them in between. Never can I get enough.

Staring blankly at him, I open the salsa, dip in a snow

pea and shove it into my mouth. "Pfft. You tell lies. I'm fat and bloated and…"

"No, you are pregnant, and your bump is beautiful." He pauses and then adds, "Just like you." He smiles at me; my insides flutter at his compliment and my heart rate accelerates. His comment and my reaction are really confusing me. I sit here, stuffing my face, and I watch him. I watch as he unpacks the bag, which has extra salsa and snow peas in it. This gesture warms my heart, leaving me feeling warm and fuzzy. Branson has gone above and beyond uncle duty since the funeral and finding out I was expecting. He's there when I have an emotional breakdown. He's been with me for each OB visit.

He's always here for me.

Always.

With this I realize how much I have taken over this life. This causes the guilt to set in; his life at the moment revolves around me and the baby. My eyes well with tears at this realization, and if Kody was still alive, he'd be doing all of this for me. Branson would be out living his life, instead he's here with an emotional, hormonal, pregnant me.

"Kase, what's wrong?" he asks, his voice laced with concern. His face etched with fear.

"Nothing…I, just…I really miss Kody," I sob, "If he were still here, he would have been the one to make this emergency trip. Instead, I've taken over your life with my demands and emotions and everything. I'm such a bad person." Tears are now cascading down my cheeks.

Through my sobs, I stuff another snow pea into my mouth and on the next whimper, the snow pea goes down the wrong way and I begin to choke. My eyes bug wide open. My cheeks turn red, it's getting harder and harder to breath.

Branson immediately races around the island and over to me. He starts hitting me on the back to dislodge the stuck snow pea but to no avail. Apart from hurting me, his hits are not doing anything to remove this damn pea stuck in my throat. Suddenly, he wraps his arms around me from behind. I stop focusing on the choking and focus on the feeling of being in his arms. The warmth emanating from his body into mine. His breath on my neck.

With one final squeeze/pull, the snow pea dislodges and I spit it onto the counter. Lifting my hand to my throat, I breathe a sigh of relief and then Branson spins me around to face him. He grips my cheeks between his palms; my eyes flip up to his. "Are you okay, Kase? Is the baby okay?"

My eyes are locked on his; they are full of worry and fright. My breathing becomes labored and it's not from the choking. I'm mesmerized by Branson's eyes—they are almost golden in this light—I could lose myself staring into them. Everything around me fades away; it reminds me of the first time that I saw Kody. Shit, Kody, thinking of him snaps me back to reality.

"Kase, are you okay?" Branson questions me again.

Stepping back from him, I nod my head and swallow. Words are eluding me right now. Blinking rapidly, I try to calm the feelings that are building within at the moment.

"Kasey!" Branson shouts.

My eyes snap back to his, "What?" I snap back.

"Are you okay?"

"I...I think so. I'm going to go lie down. Thanks for the peas," I say, before I race down the hall to my room. Closing the door, I spin around and lean back against the wood. *What was that just then?* I ask myself, lifting my hand to my mouth, I cover it and gasp. Sliding down the door, I rest my head back and rub my belly. "Fuck," I mumble.

Closing my eyes, an image of Kody flashes before me but it morphs into Branson. I feel guilty for the feelings I had a few moments ago, and now seeing him before me again, the shame and remorse I feel skyrockets. Shaking my head, I whisper, "No, no, no," over and over. Then it hits me, I don't have feelings for him, I'm just grateful he prevented me from choking to death on a snow pea. Yeah, it was feelings of gratefulness. Not lust. Not want or desire. It was thankfulness for saving my life.

Standing up, I walk over to the bed, pull the comforter back, and lie down. Rolling to my side, I get a whiff of Branson's aftershave from the pillow next to me, and those feelings from before come crashing back to me like a freight train coming down a mountain. It becomes abundantly clear to me...I'm falling in love with my dead fiancé's brother.

CHAPTER 6

Sleep eludes me for hours. My mind keeps playing over and over the feeling of being in Branson's arms. The fact I was choking to death is neither here nor there in my memories, my focus is on the warm, fuzzy, sexy feelings I felt. At one point I drift off to sleep, only to wake up some-time later with my hand in my undies, pleasuring myself. Branson's name slips from my lips as my body tenses and my self-induced orgasm detonates.

Before the sun rises, I climb out of bed, shower, and head into the office; may as well get a start on my day.

There's a knock on my door and I look up to see Chelle standing there. "Hey," I say, as she walks in and sits in the chair across from me. "How are you?"

"Tired, and you?" she says, as she leans back and stares at me.

"Getting fat," I reply and we both laugh. "What are you doing here so early?"

"Early," she questions, looking at her watch. "It's 10:15 a.m."

"What? Shit, times flies when you're having fun."

"What time did you get in?" she queries me again; her face laced with worry, but she tries to hide it with that sad fake smile people have been giving me.

"Early enough that the sun was still sleeping."

She stares at me. "Are you okay? You know you can talk to me, right? Just 'cause I'm working from home since returning from maternity leave doesn't mean I'm not here for you."

Nodding my head, I reply, "Yeah, I know. Just couldn't sleep." My mind flits to what happened when I awoke at stupid o'clock this morning…and then I start to think about my developing feelings for Branson. "Actually, can I ask you a question? It's kinda personal but pregnancy personal."

"Ask away," she says, leaning forward to listen to what I have to ask, her face serious.

"This is, umm, ahh, weird but, did you go through a phase of constantly being, umm, ahh, horny?" I whisper the last word.

Chelle bursts out laughing. "Oh my God, yes. My poor husband didn't know what hit him. Pregnancy makes you hormonally crazy." I laugh at this, as it's so very true. "Every time he looked at me I wanted to jump his bones. Never ever thought I'd hear him say, 'Honey, please, no more sex.' Never." Her face pales when she realizes where this conversation is now going. "Ohh, Kase," she says when she realizes why I'm asking. The concern on her face causes the waterworks to start. Chelle jumps up and steps around my desk, she leans on the edge. I lower my head to her lap and cry. I let it all out. I cry because I'm horny. I cry because Kody is gone. I cry over my confusion regarding Branson. I cry for everything…damn pregnancy hormones. She runs her fingers through my hair, soothing me and not saying anything. Because really, what can she say? Nothing will bring Kody back and I'm not into chicks, so she can't help with my horniness.

A knock at my door has my head pop up and peer around Chelle, it's Stacey, holding Chelle's lil' munchkin, Susan. "Everything all right?" she says, as she walks into my office and kicks the door closed behind her.

"Yep, just another pregnancy hormonal breakdown."

She eyes me suspiciously. "Well, come hold this lil' one. It will definitely put a smile on your dial."

Standing up, I walk toward her and take wee lil' Susan into my arms. As you do when you hold a baby, I put on that annoying baby voice. "Hi there, baby girl. You sure are cute." She reaches up her chubby little hand and squeezes my chin, it reminds me of Kody and my mind drifts off to a time when Kody and I were blissfully happy…

…I'm sitting in the living room watching a rerun of Fresh Prince when Kody arrives home from work. He and Branson are in the process of opening a wine bar. Aptly named, Bin 501. Looking up at him, I smile. "Hey, babe, how was your day?"

"Busy. Productive. Shattering. Tell me again why I'm doing this?"

"Because you are awesome." He places his keys on the table

by the door, kicks off his shoes, and jumps on the couch next to me. Turning to him I grin. "Hi!" I huskily say.

He leans toward me, grips my chin, and places a gentle kiss on my lips. Pulling back, he's still holding my chin and softly whispers, "I love you with all my heart and soul."

Lifting myself up, I straddle his legs, push him back into the cushion, and slam my lips against his. Our kiss quickly deepens, and before I can register what's happening, we are both naked and I'm sinking myself down on him. We rock back and forth. Just as we are both about to tumble over the orgasmic edge, he grips my cheeks and with our eyes locked on one another, we both explode, screaming each other's names as we come.

He holds my chin lovingly and runs his finger across my bottom lip as we both come down from our euphoric high…

"Earth to Kasey, hello." The sound of Stacey's voice snaps me back to reality.

Shaking my head, I smile. "Huh?"

"Where did you go just now? You are grinning like a loon."

"Just thinking about Kody," I say, my grin getting bigger.

"Man, pregnancy does crazy shit to you. Not three minutes ago, you were bawling like a baby. Now you are smiling and grinning like the Cheshire cat."

Nonchalantly, I shrug my shoulders. "What can I say, pregnancy is…"

Together, Chelle and I say, "…hormonally crazy." We both start laughing when there's a knock at my door. Through my laughter, I shout, "Come in!"

The door opens and Marlee pops her head in. "Hey."

She steps into my office with a tray of juices, a bag of snow peas, and hopefully hot salsa is in her handbag. "I come bearing gifts."

"EEEP!" I squeal in excitement, causing baby Susan to startle, "Sorry, lil' one, but Marlee here has snow peas… and hopefully salsa too."

She places the drinks tray on my desk and proceeds to pull out not one, but two jars of salsa.

"I love you, Marlee," I say, as I hand Susan over to Chelle and snatch the bag of peas from Marlee, open the bag, crack the lid on the salsa, and dive in. A moan escapes my lips and Chelle laughs.

"There's the orgasm you were chasing." My eyes bug open at what she said. Both Marlee and Stacey look between us confused. "What?" she says, confused at their blank expressions.

"What are you talking about, woman?" Marlee asks, as she takes a seat and sips on her juice.

"Nothing," I quickly cover. "Chelle is on crack this morning." I raise my eyebrows at her in a 'shut-your-mouth-they-don't-need-to-know' kind of way.

Thankfully she gets my hint because she says, "You'll understand when you are pregnant. Anyway, I must fly, this lil' one needs a nap, and I have a mountain of washing to do." She turns to face me. "You all good now?"

Nodding my head, I shove another salsa-covered pea into my mouth. "Yep, all good here." Swallowing my mouthful, I step over to her and wrap my arms around her, careful not to squish Susan. "Thank you," I whisper into her ear.

"Anytime," she whispers back. "Catch you all later." With that, she exits my office. Stacey soon follows since

she's manning reception, leaving Marlee and I to get stuck
into the planning of this year's toy drive…and it's so nice
to have Marlee on board from the beginning this year;
she's a godsend.

♡

CHAPTER 7

JULY HAS FLOWN BY, AFTER THE EXCITEMENT OF THE FOURTH, it's been busy, busy, busy. I'm nearly four months pregnant now, and my tummy is getting bigger and bigger each day. I've discovered Peanut doesn't like it when I eat peanuts, I get really bad heartburn and indigestion each time I eat them, so no more satay chicken for me.

I've just gotten home from work. Branson is coming over tonight so we can start organizing baby furniture and all the other crap that goes with babies. I'm ever so thankful to have him in my life, because it's totally overwhelming at times.

I've just slipped into a pair of linen shorts and black tank when he walks in. "Honey, I'm home." Walking down the hallway, I stop midstep when my eyes land on him. He's wearing a pair of chinos and a black, short sleeve button-down; he looks fucking edible. *Damn pregnancy hormones.*

"Hey," I say, hoping that my cheeks aren't red-hot because they feel hotter than Hades at the moment. My eyes watch as he walks into the kitchen and starts dishing up the Italian food he bought over. I'm craving mac and cheese, so this is perfect.

"Do you want some wine? I can open a bottle for you."

"Will you have a glass with me?" I eye him. "One glass won't hurt."

"Actually, that does sound nice. White okay with you?" I ask, as I open the wine fridge and grab a bottle of Verdelho out.

"Sounds perfect."

He finishes dishing up dinner and I grab two glasses, pour the wine, and set the table.

We sit down to eat and catch up on what's been happening. The evening is perfect, I can't remember the last time I was this relaxed.

Standing up, I walk into the kitchen to grab a glass of water when I stop. There's sensation in my belly I haven't felt before. "Ohh," I say.

Branson immediately jumps up and walks over to me, rubbing my back. "You okay? What wrong? I hope it wasn't the wine." His voice is laced with worry.

"I'm fine. Peanut is kicking and I really felt it just then."

"Really, can I feel?" He steps toward me and places his hand on my belly. Grabbing his hand, I move it over to the spot where I felt the kicks, but there's no movement. Glancing up at him, his face is full of excitement. My heart rate speeds up at seeing this. I swallow deeply and as I do,

Peanut kicks again. "I felt it," Branson excitedly says. "Holy crap, that's awesome."

"You should feel what it's like when she gets the hiccups."

"He gets the hiccups?"

"Yes, SHE does," I cheekily reply.

With his hand still on my belly, he stares deep into my blue eyes. "You really think Peanut is a girl?" he asks.

Shaking my head, I smile. "I've got no idea. I just like teasing you."

"Cheeky woman," he playfully replies, as he tries to tickle my side. I step back to get away and lose my balance. Branson reaches out, wraps his arm around my waist, and stops me from falling. We stare up at each other. The air around us thickens and crackles. My hand gently skims along his arm. His fingers gently rub my back. Our breathing accelerates, until the moment is broken when Branson's phone rings. We continue to stare at one another as it continues to ring. It stops ringing, only to immediately start again. "I better get that."

"Mmmhmpf," I reply, but neither of us makes a move.

Again, his phone stops ringing, and this time my phone begins to ring. "I better get that," I whisper.

He grunts an, "Mmmhmpf," but we don't move. We stay in this position, staring at one another. Branson's phone begins to ring again. "For fuck's sake," he mumbles, letting me go, he turns and grabs his phone.

Immediately, I feel the loss of his arms around me. "What?" he barks into his phone. "Sorry, mom. Hi, how are you?" I look up and he's smiling at me, I'm so confused right now. *Why am I feeling like this?*

Leaning against the counter, I lift my hand to my chest.

My heart is still beating erratically when my mind drifts off…

…In my mind, I picture Branson stalking over to me. He spins me around and bends me over the edge of the kitchen counter. Lifting my dress over my ass, he tears my panties off me, like they do in the books I read, and he slams his cock deep into me. Moaning in delight, I thrust back at him. Looking back over my shoulder, I see he has his eyes closed. He continues to thrust into me. Over and over. Harder and harder. Faster and faster. My body temperature soars and I explode around him, screaming out his name as he too reaches his climax. Both of us panting.

"Kasey!" Branson shouts, "You okay? Your cheeks are flushed."

Staring at him, I blink a few times and nod. "Yeah, I'm good. Think the wine went to my head." *Yeah, good save.* "I'm going to sit down. Is that okay?"

"Yeah, sure. Sit down. I'll clean this up and make you some tea."

Nodding my head, I walk over to the sofa and take a seat. Tucking my legs under me, I rest a hand on my chest. My heart is still beating fast but not as fast as before in my dream. Staring into space, I play the daydream over and over. Lifting my hand to my mouth, I cover it and whisper, "Fuck."

I'm still off in Lalaland when Branson sits beside me. He places his hand on my belly and once again Peanut kicks. His face lights up with joy, and he leans toward my belly. "Hey, Peanut. I'm Uncle Branson, we can't wait to meet you. I'm sorry you won't get to meet your daddy, but

I promise to tell you a different story about him each and every day. He would have loved you sooo much. I'm sorry you won't get to meet him, he was pretty awesome, but that makes you awesome by default." Branson looks up at me and winks. "And your mommy is pretty awesome too."

Placing my hand over Branson's, we spend the rest of the night talking to my belly and telling Peanut stories about Kody. The awkwardness of earlier and my inappropriate thoughts have disappeared, and we are back to our usual Branson and Kasey.

Just before midnight, Branson heads home and I climb into bed. Immediately, I drift off to sleep but a few hours later, my eyes snap open, my body is covered in sweat, and tingling from my dream climax. My chest is heaving as I struggle to breathe. "I just had another erotic dream about Branson," I whisper to myself. Lifting my hand to my chest, I focus on my breathing until it returns to normal. "Fuck," I mumble as I think about what just transpired in my dream.

CHAPTER 8

THE DAYS ARE FLYING BY, IT'S MID-SEPTEMBER AND I'M currently five months pregnant. My belly is getting bigger and bigger each day, I feel like I'm the size of a whale whose eaten a Megalodon. I'm pretty sure I waddle like a duck when I walk—this was confirmed when Chloe and Gage both quacked at me when I walked past the break room earlier today. My feet and ankles are swollen and I'm horny as hell…all-the-freakin'-time. My mind is in a constant state of arousal, damn pregnancy hormones. My dreams always star Branson and they are off the charts hot; I wake up soaked and tingling all over. The dreams are happening more and more often, and they're becoming more and more X-rated. Dream sex with Branson, is fantastic…*I wonder what actual sex with him would be like?*

I'm sitting in Gage's office for a meeting but once again, my mind drifts off to sexy land with Branson. I'm snapped back to reality when I hear Gage saying something about pink and blue aliens. "What?" I snap.

"I knew you weren't listening."

"Was too," I snarkily retort.

"Okay, what did I just say?"

"Advertising spots for the holidays are nearly full… and something about aliens."

"Lucky guess. Now, want to tell me what's on your mind? You've been off with the fairies for weeks now. I put it down to your pregnancy, but I think it's more."

"It's nothing," I say, flicking at an imaginary piece of lint on my work pants.

"Is it Branson?" My eyes flick to his, and my cheeks darken.

"How did you know?"

"I have eyes and you change when he's around. Wanna talk about it?"

"There's nothing to talk about. He's my baby's uncle. My financé's brother. There's nothing else to say about him." He eyes me. "Okay, fine. I can't stop thinking about him. I've been having super steamy, X-rated dreams about him, but I keep telling myself it's just pregnancy hormones. Chelle said it happens…but I…" I drift off, I don't finish what I was going to say because it hits me like a ton of bricks; *I'm in love with Branson.* "No, Gage, no," I say as jump up shaking my head. "I can't be in love with Branson, I can't be. He's Kody's brother for fuck's sake. He's Peanut's uncle." Leaning my arms on Gage's desk, I hang my head as a tear falls down my cheek. My lip quivers, I step back and fall down into the chair. *How can I be falling in love with my dead fiancé's brother?* "No. No. No," I mumble through my tears.

Gage stands up, walks around his desk, and takes the chair next to me. He rests his hand on my knee. "Kase, look at me." Lifting my gaze to his, I stare blankly at him. "Do you remember last Christmas when I fell in love with Marlee?" I nod as the memory comes back to me and I smile. "I remember a conversation I had with you and Kody. It was the day I realized I was in love with her. Kody said, 'There is no rhyme or reason when it comes to love. It happens when you least expect it. It happens with a person that never in your wildest dreams you think it would. No one can control love, just go with it. Everyone deserves love.' Kase, I know, he'd tell you exactly that if he was still here." He pauses and then adds, "He'd be happy for you and Branson."

"But his brother?" I whine.

"Buttercup." I glare at him because I hate when he calls me that. "I don't know what else to say, but I knew Kody, and he'd want you to be happy. Both of you."

"I know he would, but his brother? What the fuck is wrong with me?"

"Nothing, except for your snow pea and salsa obsession. That shit is just wrong."

"Have you tried it?" I snap.

He shakes his head at me. "Nope, no way in hell."

"Then shut it and help me figure this Branson thing out."

"What's there to figure out? You like him. He likes you. Someone needs to make a move."

"But what if he doesn't like me? What if he just thinks of me as his sort of sister-in-law? And he's just being nice 'cause I'm kinda his family!"

"Trust me, he doesn't," he matter-of-factly replies. "He like you just as much, if not more."

"How do you know what?"

"I have eyes. You two are gaga for each other but neither is willing to make a move because of Kody. But Kody isn't here, and I know for a fact, he would want you both to be happy. Sure, it's a little unconventional but love is love."

"When did you become so…so girly?"

"When I crashed into a black-haired, blue-eyed angel who took my breath away."

"Fuck, you make me sick. Speaking of Marlee, how's she doing?"

"She's great. We are great. Everything is great."

"That's great," I cheekily say, but deep down it hurts that he's so great. So happy and in love, and I'm over here pregnant, grieving and possibly in love with someone who I shouldn't be. *Fuck my life*, I think to myself.

"I've got to head to a meeting, but Marlee will be by later today to work on the drive again. Maybe talk to her. Get a woman's perspective."

"Yeah, maybe. I'll think about it. Speaking of the drive, can we count on you to be Santa again?"

"Yes," he groans, but deep down, I know he loved playing Santa last year.

"From what I heard, you loooooved playing Santa last year." His eyes snap to mine and his cheeks turn pink with embarrassment. "No worries, naughty Nick, your secret is safe with me…for now." Standing up, I exit Gage's office. Spinning back, I poke my head inside. "Thanks Gage. I appreciate the pep talk."

"Anytime, Buttercup, anytime."

Sticking my tongue at him, I make my way back to my office, thinking about what Gage and I just discussed.

The rest of the afternoon went by in a blur, I have no idea what I did. And I have no idea what Marlee and I finalized for the drive. When quitting time rolls around, I'm ever so thankful because I'm shattered.

The drive home took forever due to an accident on the freeway, and as I'm walking up the stairs, my mind once again drifts to Branson and my ever-growing feelings. Does he feel the same way about me too? Or is this just horny pregnancy hormones messing with my head?

When I open my front door, I have my answer.

CHAPTER 9

STEPPING INSIDE, I PAUSE MIDSTEP. BEFORE ME IS A GORGEOUS romantic dinner. Branson is standing by the table, and I can see in his eyes that he's wondering if it's too much, "Branson, it's…"

"It's too much, I know. But I wanted to do something special for you."

"Branson, thank you, it's perfect," I say, as I walk over to him and wrap my arms around his waist, resting my head on his chest. The sound of his heartbeat calms my erratically beating one. I sigh and take a deep breath. My senses are assaulted with dinner and Branson. I find myself smiling, and when he runs his hands innocently up my back, it sends shock waves directly between my thighs…and for once, I don't think it is pregnancy hormones, it's all Branson. Gage's words from earlier come flooding back to me.

Lifting my head, I look up at him and wonder if he feels the same way about me too. Could Gage be right? Does he have the same feelings as me? We stare at each other for a few moments before he pulls away. "Let's eat."

"Yep," I reply, letting the 'p' pop. Walking over to the table, I dejectedly take a seat and watch Branson dish up. As I watch him scoop pasta and sauce onto our plates, I begin to think he doesn't seem to like me in the way I like him; well I think I like him…damn Gage and his advice. Then it hits me—I do like him—and the idea he doesn't like me, the way I like him, sends a knife straight through my heart.

Pushing my chair back from the table, I race down the hall. "B-Be right back," I stutter as the first tear falls, closing the door to my bedroom, I slide down the door, rest my head on the wood, and silently cry. Sniffing in the most unladylike way, I begin to laugh—damn hormones. Here I am, crying over my dead fiancé's brother not liking me one minute, and the next, I'm laughing because I like my dead fiancé's brother.

A knock on the door startles me. "You okay, Kase?"

"Yeah, just a pregnancy hormone moment. Give me a sec and I'll be out."

"Okay," he says through the door, his voice laced with worry and concern.

Standing up, I walk into the en suite and splash water on my face. Taking a deep breath, I head back out to face Branson. He's sitting at the table with his back to me. My heart flutters when I see him, he must sense my presence because he turns his head toward me. When he smiles, my heart does a somersault in my chest and I find myself grinning back at him.

"Sorry about that," I say, as I walk over to the table and take a seat next to him, resting my hands on the table.

He takes my hand in his and squeezes. "No apologies necessary, but are you sure you're okay?"

Nodding my head, I smile. "Yeah, I'm fine. Tired but fine."

"Well, after dinner, you rest on the couch and I'll clean up."

Shaking my head, no, I point my finger at him. "Uhh, uh, mister. You cooked therefore I clean. House rules."

"When have I ever listened to house rules? Or rules for that matter?"

Staring at him, I try and hide back my smirk. "Well, umm…"

"Yeah, that's what I thought too. After dinner, you rest. I clean."

"You going all caveman on me, Mr. Holmes?"

"If that's what it takes for you to rest up, then yes."

We stare at one another. It's intense but at the same time calming. "Fine, but your punishment for cleaning up will be to watch whatever I want on Netflix."

"Deal." He outstretches his hand for me to shake and agree on the plan. Placing my hand in his, an electrical current zaps through me; from the look on his face, he feels it too. We stare at each other for a few more seconds before he says, "Let's eat."

We pick up our forks and dig into the pasta. And like always, we fall into easy conversation with a few laughs, just like it's natural. My eyes keep drifting over to him and I swear on a few occasions, I catch him staring at me too… maybe Gage is right and he does feel something for me as well…or it's wishful thinking on my behalf. But as with everything to do with us, there's Kody—he's the invisible giant elephant in the room.

Wiping my mouth on my napkin, I sit back and rest my hands on my belly, "Dude, that was amazing."

"It was my pleasure." He takes a sip of his wine and stares at me. "I like seeing you smile like that."

"I like smiling this this," I breath in deeply and then add, "I like *you* making me smile like this."

Without missing a beat, he replies, "I like *making* you smile."

We stare at each other for a few moments. The silence is oddly comfortable. Branson leans toward me and I think—hope—he's going to kiss me, when he grabs the plate in front of me. "I'll get to these dishes." And just like that, the moment is gone and we are back Kasey and Branson, almost brother and sister-in-law.

While Branson cleans up, I move over to the couch and position myself so I have a clear view of the kitchen…and Branson…and easy access to my snow peas and salsa. While I watch him, a warm, fuzzy feeling envelops me, I like seeing him in the kitchen. Every now and then, he'll glance over to me, totally catching me watching him, and he'll wink or stick his tongue out at me. It's fun and light-hearted…it's perfect.

Now I just need to grow some lady balls and tell him how I feel. There are sooo many things holding me back, but my biggest concern is I'll scare him off and I need him in my life. I can't do this without him. Maybe I need to sacrifice my happiness to ensure Peanut has the best possible life.

"What ya thinking about?"

"Shit." I jump in fright; I hadn't even realized he'd

finished with the kitchen and was now sitting next to me. He lifts my legs and places them on his thighs. He grabs my foot and begins to massage it. "MMMMMM," I moan. "It feels so good."

Opening my eyes, I see him staring intently at me, the rich brown of his eyes like dark chocolate. My heart rate increases, my mouth becomes dry. The air around us thickens as we continue to stare at one another.

Lifting my legs off him, I shuffle so I'm sitting next to him. We both turn and cross our legs, facing one another. He reaches over and takes my hands in his. Lifting them to his lips, he places a gentle kiss on my knuckles. My heart stops beating this time, we both lean toward one another. Our breathing hurried, my chest rising erratically with each breath. I can feel his warm breath on my face, my eyes close and I wait for it…but it never comes.

Opening my eyes, I see Branson has pulled back. He quickly hops up. "I have to go, busy day tomorrow." He leans down, places a kiss on my forehead, and quickly leaves. Leaving me sitting here alone.

Rejected.

Relieved.

All of the above.

"What the fuck?" I murmur to the room, covering my mouth with my hand, letting out a frustrated sigh.

Now I'm even more confused than before. Shaking my head, I stand up, turn all the lights off, and head to bed. After changing into my pajamas, I lie on the mattress and stare at the ceiling. Sleep eludes me. I keep playing the scene from earlier over and over in my head. He wanted to kiss me—I know he did—but why did he pull away, why? Is it shame for wanting his dead brother's fiancée? Is he revolted by my pregnant body? Or are my pregnancy hormones in overdrive, making me think there's something there when there's not?

"Gah!" I shout to the room, smacking the bedsheets in frustration.

Climbing out of bed, I walk into the kitchen, grab my snow peas and salsa, and sit at the island counter and munch away.

My phone dings with a text; grabbing it, my heart stops when I see it's from Branson.

Branson: *I'm sorry about earlier. Can I take you to dinner on Friday night?*

He wants to take me out. Is this a date? Or an 'I'm sorry but I'm just not that into you' dinner? Either way, I want to find out.

Kasey: *I'd like that.*
Branson: *It's a date. Pick you up at 7*
Branson: *Nite nite :)*
Kasey: *Looking forward to it. Nite Xo*

Once again I'm confused about everything when it comes to Branson, but at the same time, I can't wait for our date/non-date on Friday. One way or another, I'm going to find out how Branson really feels about me…and I really hope we are on the same page.

CHAPTER 10
BRANSON

My dinner invitation was meant to be a friendly, 'I'm sorry for almost kissing you, we are still great friends, please don't hate me' dinner,' but then I had to go and text back 'it's a date.' *What the fuck, Holmes?* But at the same time, I'm happy she said yes, maybe I haven't ruined us after all.

THE NEXT THREE DAYS DRAG. I'M A CRANKY ASSHOLE TO everyone and I've steered clear of Kasey's place for fear of doing something stupid…like trying to kiss her again… even though I really, really want to kiss her. To feel her lips pressed against mine. To run my hands over her sexy body. To feel my dick slide into her wet heat, fuck, I need to stop thinking about this, otherwise I'm going to have to jack off…again.

Even though I'm not seeing her, each day after work I head over to her place and watch. I sit in my car like a creeper and keep an eye on her house. More than anything, I want to get out of my car, go inside, and see how she's doing, but I'm too chicken to go in and see her. I'm fearful that our almost moment from the other night has ruined everything between us.

Finally it's Friday, I'm a ball of nerves all day. I feel like I'm going to throw up. Holy shit, I'm going on a fucking date with Kasey Wellson.

My dead brother's fiancée.

The mother of his child.

My 'ish sister-in-law.

I'm totally going to hell for this, but it will be so worth it.

Any pain associated in relation to spending time with and falling for Kasey will totally be worth any punishment thrown my way. If I'm honest, I've been in love with Kasey for as long as Kody has—well, a few moments longer—and I remember the day we first met her, like it was yesterday…

…Kody and I were having a few beers in the bar around the corner from U of I, the door opened and I swear my heart stopped beating. In walked the most stunning woman I had ever seen. Her chocolate brown locks were blowing in the wind. She had vivid blue eyes that I could clearly see from where I was sitting. Curves in all the right places. Perfect pert breasts, encased in an emerald green sweater that fit her like a glove. Legs that went on and on and her jeans looked like they were painted on. I was snapped back to reality when Kody, slapped me on the back. "You want another, dude?"

"Huh?" I deadpanned.

"You want another beer?" he repeated.

"Yeah, sure okay," I said, shaking my head, I looked back to the door but the goddess from before had disappeared.

The hairs on the back of my neck prickled, I turned in my seat, and she was walking toward me: the angel from before. Kody was behind her, he had the goofiest grin on his face, and I knew he saw her. "Just here," he said to her, pointing to the table and me. "Branson, this is Kasey and her friend, Chloe. Kasey, Chloe, this is my brother, Branson."

"Hi," both the girls said but my eyes were locked on Kasey. She was even more stunning up close. She smiled at me, and I felt it deep in my soul. She then turned her attention to Kody and I was forgotten. The two of them hit it off immediately, and soon they were inseparable. I became the third wheel, but I'd happily be the third wheel if it meant I could be near Kasey. That is until one day Kody told me to back off, he wanted to get serious with Kasey and I was not welcome anymore.

I'd never seen my brother so enamored with someone before, so I did the brotherly thing and I backed off. His, and her, happiness meant more to me than my own, so I stepped back and watched as the two of them fell hopelessly in love with one another and planned their life together…

Shaking that memory away, I finish getting ready for my non-date date with Kasey. After my trip down memory lane, I'm excited to see what happens tonight, but at the same time, I feel guilty for pursuing her now. Sure, I stepped back and let Kody have her in the beginning, but he's not here—man that makes me sound like an asshole— and I am. Kasey deserves to be happy. She deserves to be loved once again. This is a fucked-up situation but for once, I want to put me first. I want to see if there is anything there between us, and if these last few weeks are anything to go by, the dynamics between us have changed, a few almost kisses. Innocent touches here and there. We've had a few 'moments' as they'd say in the movies, and I'm at the point where I want those moments to move forward. I think Kody would be happy for us. I know if it was me; I would be but at the same time, how will our families feel about it all? How will others feel?

This is a fucked-up situation but I don't give a damn, I want Kasey Wellson and I'm going to go for it. Consequences be damned.

CHAPTER 11

I'm a ball of nerves as I wait for Branson to pick me up, I seriously have first date nerves even though this isn't a date date...well, I don't think it is, but his text did say 'it's a date.' But that phrase can be interpreted in many ways. GAH, I hate this. Why can't things just go back to me being fat and pregnant and Branson being uncle to Peanut, not Branson being the star of my X-rated fantasies, or my future.

Before I can work myself up any further, there's a knock at the door. That in itself is weird, and then I start fretting all over again. Waddling to the door, I swing it open and both our mouths drop open. Branson is wearing a black button-down shirt, the sleeves rolled up to his elbows, and dark denim jeans that I'm sure are hugging his ass perfectly.

"WOW, you look stunning," Branson says, looking down I see my big belly encased in emerald green from my halter dress, one of the few dresses that still fit me.

"Thanks, you look pretty good yourself," I reply, brushing my hair behind my ear, just for something to do with my hands, otherwise I'd reach out, grip his cheeks, and slam my lips against his. Hearing Branson say my name, snaps me back to the present. "Huh?"

"Are you ready to go?"

Nodding my head. "Yep, just let me grab my purse."

Spinning around, I walk to the hall table and grab my bag, I swear I hear him whisper, 'fuck, she's gorgeous' and when I turn back around, I find Branson staring intently at me. "Let's go," I say, as I walk toward him.

Locking the door, he places his hand on my lower back and we walk toward his car. He applies just enough pressure to let me know his hand is there, but not too much that he's really touching me. It feels amazing and when he removes his hand, to open the car door for me, I feel the loss of his touch and I deflate a little.

Climbing in, I click my belt into the buckle and watch as Branson climbs in, starts the car, and we head to the restaurant. The car ride is silent, it's slightly awkward, but it gives me time to watch him. I can see he's just as nervous as I am. Seeing that confuses me even more, and I get my hopes up that he does want what I want, and it's not just my imagination…or pregnancy hormones running rampant.

We pull up at the restaurant and the valet opens my door for me. Taking his hand, I not-so-gracefully lift myself out of the car. Stepping to the curb, I wait for Branson. He hands his keys to the valet and walks over to me. Without saying anything, I link my arm with his and we walk into the restaurant.

The hostess greets us, "Welcome to Valentino's."

"Hi, I have a reservation for Holmes, Branson Holmes," Branson says and I giggle. He looks over to me. "What's so funny?"

"You just did your name like James Bond, you better order a martini tonight to keep up the rouse," I playfully reply.

In a really, really bad Bond accent he says, "Shaken, not stirred."

We look at each other before we both burst out laughing. Peanut must think it's fun too because she kicks me violently. "Ohh!" I complain, pressing my hand to my stomach.

"Are you okay?"

"Fine. But I don't think Peanut liked your impression, she just kicked me violently in the ribs."

Dropping to his knees, my heart stops, then he places his hands on my belly and whispers, "Sorry, Peanut, I promise no more impressions."

Branson looks up at me and winks, before he stands back up and takes my hand in his, kissing my knuckles. The feeling of his lips against my skin causes it to prickle and my body to zing to life. My cheeks darken with desire and I smile back at him. The moment is broken when our hostess interrupts us, "Your table is ready, please follow me."

I hadn't even noticed she had disappeared, so we follow her to our table. Branson pulls my chair out and I sit down. He places a kiss on my temple and then takes his seat across from me.

The night flies by and I can't remember a time when I laughed so much. All the worries I had about our non-date date were for nothing. The night was perfect in every possible way…until Branson tried to eat some of my chocolate lava cake. "Uhh, uh, mister." I smack his hand away. "If you wanted dessert you should have ordered dessert. Now back off and let me lose myself in this choco-latey goodness."

Digging the spoon in, I lift it to my mouth, and moan as the chocolate and sauce hit my taste buds. When I open my eyes, Branson is staring at me. I can feel his gaze deep in my bones. The moment is broken when Peanut viciously kicks me again. "Uhh," I moan, leaning forward.

Branson is immediately out of his seat and by my side. "Are you okay? Peanut?"

Nodding my head, I grab his hand and place it on my belly. Before I can say anything, Peanut kicks again. "Holy shit, that was a big one."

"Yeah, she's been doing that all day."

"He's a strong one," he cheekily replies.

A woman, walking past, stops and smiles at us both. "You two make a gorgeous couple, good luck with the munchkin."

We stare at her as she leaves, Branson turns and gazes at me. We both smile at one another, until I flinch again from Peanut's football antics.

"Let's get you home," Branson says as he stands up. He then offers his hand to me and I willingly take it. Lacing our fingers together, we walk to the front, settle the bill, and head home.

On the car ride back to my place, it's silent but it gives

me time to think. Should I make a move on Branson? Should I not, and leave our relationship, or whatever we have as it is? Then I start to think about the negatives. He's Kody's brother. What will everyone think?

Before I've made a decision, we arrive home. Branson gets out and walks around the hood before he opens my door. He outstretches his hand to help me out. "Thanks," I shyly say, when both my feet are safely on the driveway. We silently walk over to the front door. Digging my keys out, I unlock the door but instead of opening it and going inside, I turn to face him and I smile. "Thank you for a lovely evening."

"My pleasure, Kase. I had a great time too." He pauses and then adds, "I always have a great time when I'm with you."

My knees wobble at this and my insides turns to mush. That's the most romantic thing I have heard in ages. Stepping over to him, I wrap my arms around his waist and rest my head on his chest. He envelops me in his arms and hugs me back. Closing my eyes, I lose myself to the feeling of being in his arms. I breathe in his scent and find myself smiling. Without thinking, I lift my head and place my lips gently on his.

We are both frozen. Neither one of us moves; that is until my brain kicks in and I pull back. "Umm, ahh, good night," I quickly say. Spinning on my heel, I open the door and race inside. Slamming it shut behind me, I race into my bedroom and collapse onto the bed and let the tears pour down my cheeks. Through my sobs, I whisper, "I'm sorry, Kody. I didn't mean to kiss him." Then I sit upright and add, "Yes I did, Kody, I love Branson. What am I going to do?"

Another avalanche of tears cascades down my cheeks, I

curl onto my side and rub my belly. Eventually I drift off to sleep and my last thought before I drift off to sleep is Branson…and he's my first thought when I wake the next morning too.

$$\heartsuit$$

CHAPTER 12

For the next week, things between Branson and I are different. It's not awkward per se, but it's definitely not as easy as it has been in the past. No longer do we have a fun carefree relationship, instead it's strained and different, I'm not used to walking on eggshells around him.

Once again, sleep eludes me, because every time I close my eyes, I dream sexy naughty things about Branson. These damn pregnancy hormones are driving me crazy, sex crazy. It's times like this I really wish Kody were still alive, because I'd mount him like a cowboy and ride him hard.

It's 4:26 a.m. and I'm wide-awake, so I climb out of bed. Walking down the hallway, I stop at the door to Kody's office. Stepping inside, I flick on the light switch and glance around the room. I wonder if I should turn his office into the nursery, or maybe use the room across the hall. Both are centrally located from the bedroom and the main living area. This room is a little bigger which is the only reason I'm considering it, but at the same time, I don't want to disturb this room either. This was Kody's room, his man cave and I'm not sure I'm ready to do that, but I know I have to. Peanut will be here before I know it and I know Kody would have chosen this room for him.

Stepping over to his desk, I sit down in his chair. When I do, a waft of Kody's scent permeates the air. Every now and again I'll do something and I can smell him. This time, I smile rather than cry. Leaning back in the chair, I rub my ever-growing belly. "Peanut, your daddy is giving up his office for you. He would have given up anything for you. Just like I'd give anything to have him here. Luckily, Uncle Branson is here. He's pretty awesome, you'll love him lots and lots. Just like m—" I don't finish that out loud, because my love for him is just crazy pregnancy hormones. Hell, I haven't had sex since before I flew to Kansas for my bachelorette party. Tears well in my eyes because it was a super quick quickie before I flew out. Kody and I hardly ever had quickies; we always took our time. Exploring every inch of each other's body. There wasn't a spot that we hadn't explored.

Wiping away the tears, I clench my thighs together. I'm so fucking horny right now. Subconsciously, I lift my hand and trace my fingers across my chest, circling my nipples through my nightie. They immediately pebble and the pulsing sensation between my thighs becomes stronger. Gripping my breasts, I gently massage them, biting my lip and losing myself to the sensation. One hand continues to caress and massage my breast, while the other dips between my thighs, rubbing myself over the top of my cotton panties. The material is soaked as I push it aside and trace up and down my slit. Leaning to the side, I lean on the arm of the chair and moan as I slip a digit between my swollen, wet lips. Sliding my finger in and out, I grasp the chair arm, my breaths coming hard and fast. That fluttering feeling begins to build. When I press my thumb against my clit, I reach my crescendo and scream as I tumble over the edge, thrusting my finger in and out, my pussy walls clenching as I ride out my climax.

Removing my hand, I lean back in my chair and catch my breath. Closing my eyes, an image of Branson flashes before me and I sit upright, opening them quickly as a wave of guilt crashes into me. I should be thinking of Kody when I masturbate, not his brother.

Standing up, I walk over to his bookshelves and I run my fingers along the book spines. Picking up a wooden box I hadn't paid any attention to before, I lift the lid and gasp when I see a couple of envelopes sitting there. The top one has my name on it in Kody's handwriting. Turning to the desk, I place the box down and take out the envelopes. There are two, one for me and one for Branson.

Sitting down at the desk again, I stare at the envelopes I placed on the desk. I'm still staring at them when I hear Branson open the front door and come in. Even with what's going on between us, he still checks on me each and every morning before he heads into to the bar.

Glancing out the window, I realize the sun is now up and I have been sitting here, staring at the envelopes for a few hours now.

"Kase, you awake?" Branson yells.

"In here," I reply, as I pick up the envelopes. My eyes locked on them in my hands. I feel Branson's presence before I see him, and when I look up, he's leaning against the doorframe staring at me, sitting at Kody's desk.

"What are you doing in here?" he asks, but I don't answer him, I keep staring at the envelopes in my hand. "Kase, you okay?" he asks, stepping into the room and around the desk. He leans against the wood and stares down at me. I can feel his gaze on me, but I can't stop looking at my hands. Kody's beautiful penmanship staring up at me.

"Kase," he says again.

This time, I stare up and whisper, "He wrote us each a letter."

"What?" He eyes flick to my hands. His mouth drops open when he recognizes the writing on them. "What? How? Where did you find these?"

"In the box on the shelf. I don't know why I opened it this morning. I just did, and then I found these."

"What do they say?" he asks.

Shaking my head sideways, I shrug. "Don't know. I've been staring at them for the last few hours. Not brave enough to open mine and read it." Lifting his, I hand it to him. "This one's yours."

He takes the envelope from me, and our fingers brush, a spark zapping through me. My eyes flick up to his and I know he felt it too.

"Should we read them?" he asks.

"Guess so."

"Come on," he says, outstretching his hand to me. I place my hand in his; he pulls me up, kisses my forehead, and leads me out to the living room. We take a seat on the couch, and I pull my legs under me. Once again staring at the envelope.

I'm scared to open it but at the same time, I want to

know what Kody has to say. Taking a deep breath, I say, "Let's do this."

Without taking another minute, I open the envelope and pull out a single piece of paper. As soon as I see his handwriting, my eyes well with tears. Taking another deep breath, I read.

My dearest Kasey,

If you are reading this, then our plans went to shit and I'm gone…but know I'll be watching you from above and looking over you, especially when you are in the shower.

You were the best thing to ever happen to me and I had the best life with you. Now that I'm gone, I want you to move on. I want you to be happy. I want you to get your happily ever after.

I will always love you, and I know you will forever love me too, but your heart is big enough to love again, and I want that more than anything. You deserve to love and be loved.

Branson will need a shoulder to cry on, be that person for him. Be his person, like he was always mine. Actually, you two would be perfect together, but I'm just lucky I bumped into your first.

Kasey, my love, my one and only. I'm sorry I left you before our time, but know in the time I had with you, I was happier than a pig in shit.

You will always have my heart.

I love you with my heart and soul, always and forever.

Yours always,

Kody

I've finished reading and my eyes are now leaking profusely. Tears are pouring down my face at his words. It's like he knew he was going to die and I would develop feelings for Branson. He foresaw the future and knew what was going to happen. Looking over to Branson, I see he's still reading.

Reaching out, I squeeze his hand. He looks up at me and sadly smiles, his eyes glassy with unshed tears.

"I need to read it again," he whispers. He stands up and walks into the kitchen. His back to me, he turns and leans against the counter. His lips move as he reads his letter for a second time.

Branson,
My brother, my best friend, if you are reading this then I've kicked the bucket and I'm in heaven surrounded by angels and an abundance of wine and cheese #Winning, but seriously, I'm sorry I left you behind. I know we've done everything together, but this was one journey I had to take alone.
You were a great brother, the best anyone could ask for in fact. You were a fantastic friend and an absolutely brilliant business partner. I love you, Branson. We never said that much when I was alive, but it's true.
I ask only one thing, please look after Kasey for me. I know she will struggle when I'm gone, but deep down she's tough and with a push in the right direction, she will love again. Actually, you two would be perfect together. You've both always had a close bond, and I know you will be there for her. I'm glad I bumped into her first, because one conversation with you, and I would have lost her to you. I want her to be happy more than

anything, and I'm giving you that task to make sure it happens. <u>Don't fuck it up.</u>
Cheers,
Kody

When he's finished reading his letter for the second time, he looks over at me. Something passes between us when our eyes meet. Swallowing deeply, I know whatever was in his letter is similar to mine, and we have Kody's blessing. A force takes over my body; I stand up from the sofa and walk toward him. He pushes off the counter and does the same, walking toward me. We meet in the middle of the room; he takes my hands in his and squeezes them reassuringly. Dropping my hands, he grips my cheeks and stares intently into my eyes. My heart is beating erratically, like it wants to jump out of my chest. I'm nervous yet excited at the same time. He lowers his head and leans toward me, and I lean into him and wrap my arms around his waist. Our lips connect and an electrical current passes through my body, from head to toe. Closing my eyes, I open my mouth slightly and he slides his tongue inside. Our tongues dance together, our lips fused to one another. Gently pulling me to him, he slips one hand up into my hair and the other around my shoulders, holding me close to him.

This kiss is electric.

This kiss is everything I imagined and more.

It's the perfect first kiss.

Breaking the connection, I pull back and stare at him, my chest rapidly rising and falling. His stare penetrates deep into my soul and I know: this is right. Taking his hand in mine, I lead him down the hall toward the bedroom.

What happens next will change everything between us, but after reading Kody's letter, I can't wait anymore. I want this. I need this. I need Branson like I need my next breath. I need him in every possible way and Kody knew I would. Now that I have Kody's blessing, I can't wait to see what happens next.

CHAPTER 13

We enter the bedroom and stop at the end of the bed; I turn to face Branson. My eyes roam over his body before landing on his face, his beautiful perfect face. Lifting my hand, I cup his cheek. "Branson," I whisper.

He wraps an arm around my waist and pulls me to him; he lowers his lips to mine and kisses me again. Closing my eyes, I give myself over to him and the kiss. Never have I been kissed like this before. I thought the kiss before was magnificent, but this kiss trumps that one.

Breaking the connection, he stares into my eyes. His gaze drops to my lips. "You have the lips of an angel, Kasey." He kisses me again and again; I feel each kiss deep in my soul. He then nuzzles down my neck and rakes his hand down my side. "You have a sinfully sexy body, and

I'm going to explore every inch of it with my tongue." He lifts my nightie over my head, leaving me only in my panties. He grins when he sees my breasts exposed. Lowering his head, his tongue flicks my nipple and I moan. He sucks the tight bud into his mouth, and I throw my head back in ecstasy. He gently bites the tip before letting it pop free, that nip causes my body to shudder. Never have I reacted to a man this way before.

Staring into his eyes, I murmur, "Make love to me, Branson."

He pauses and stares at me, a jolt of fear courses through me but it was for nothing when he grabs his shirt behind his neck and lifts it over his head, throwing it on top of my nightgown. Lifting my hand, I trace between his pectorals, down his abs, and circle his navel. His skin prickles with goosebumps. My fingers reach his pants and I fumble with his button and fly. He places his hand over mine. "Let me." Quickly he removes his pants. He's standing before me in only his boxer briefs, and I can clearly see the outline of his cock—his very hard thick cock—and I lick my lips. Dragging my teeth across my bottom lip, I slide my hand inside his briefs and grip his cock. It throbs beneath my touch, Branson groans. His groan causes my clit to throb and I moan.

He grins at me and lifts his hand to rub between my legs, my panties dampening at his touch. My pussy zinging to life. Except from Buzz and my hand, she's seen no male contact in a few months and his fingers are heaven. *I can only imagine what his cock is going to feel like.*

Stepping back, I sit on the edge of the bed and scoot up to the top. Lifting my hand, I beckon him toward me with my finger. He kneels on the end of the mattress and gazes down on me. His eyes are ablaze with lust. Skimming my finger across my chest, I circle my nipple, as his eyes track my finger's movement.

Raising my leg, he kisses my ankle. Every so slowly, working his way up my leg, he reaches the juncture between my thighs, he breathes in deeply, "MMMMM," he groans before lowering his lips to my panty-covered pussy and sucking. My hips buck, thrusting myself farther into him. He pulls the material to the side and licks up my slit, circling his tongue over my clit. Again my hips lift off the bed and I moan. Pleasure courses through my body as he continues to lick me; I'm close to coming when suddenly he stops.

Gripping my panties, he tugs them down my legs. I'm now naked and never in my thirty years have I felt so sexy. "Please, Branson," I beg.

He nods at me as he quickly removes his briefs, settling between my legs. He lines his cock up at my entrance, his eyes locked with mine. He slowly enters me, my eyes close at the intrusion. "Open your eyes, baby. I want to see the look in your eyes when I'm fully inside of you." My eyes snap open and I stare up at him.

He pushes in, and I struggle to keep my eyes open. Never have I felt so full, he pulls out and gently thrusts back in. He stares down at me as he continues to slide in and out. I want nothing more than to kiss him right now, but my baby bump prevents that. My walls clench around him and I know I'm almost there.

"I'm close," I whimper.

This spurs him on and he increases his thrusts. He grunts. I moan. My hands lift to my chest and when I tug on my nipple, I explode. Crying out as my body tenses, a violent orgasm detonates. My vision blurs and I scream as the final explosion rips through me. Branson freezes, his hips shuddering as he comes inside of me.

His body stills, his chest heaving. He stares down at me and grins. Pulling out, he collapses next to me and we roll to our sides, facing one another. He cups my cheek and gently kisses me. My eyes close, I wrap my arm around him and kiss him back. Breaking the kiss, I stare at him and smile. For the first time in a long time, I feel free. Happy. Content.

The moment is broken when the baby kicks. Branson's eyes pop wide open. "Did he just kick me?"

"Looks like *SHE* did," I reply. Grabbing his hand, I roll to my back and place his palm on my belly. My hand over his as Peanut kicks and kicks.

"I'll never get sick of feeling this," Branson says.

Turning my head to look up at him, I smile. For a moment I hesitate and then think stuff it. "Branson, I love you."

His face lights up. "I love you too, Kasey."

Rolling to my side, I kiss him. Pushing up, I straddle him and pull him into a sitting position. We wrap our arms around each other and kiss; our hands roaming each other's bodies. Between us, I feel his cock twitch. Reaching down, I stroke his cock until he's hard again. Lifting onto my knees, I sink down on him and begin to rock back and forth. He leans down and takes a nipple into his mouth, my head drops back, and I lose myself to the pleasure. A few thrust later, we both come, murmuring each other's names into our kiss.

Easing off Branson, I snuggle into his side; we quietly lie in each other's arms for a few moments when he suddenly climbs out. Intently, I watch his sexy ass as he bends down and pulls his phone from his pants. He calls the bar and says he won't be in today. After hanging up, he winks at me and climbs back into bed.

We spend the day naked, wrapped up in each other. We chat. We make love several times. We laugh. We plan for the future. We are happier than we have been since we lost Kody.

Later that evening, we eat pizza in bed for dinner and ravish each other for dessert. We blissfully drift off to sleep, wrapped in each other's embrace, and for the first time in weeks, I don't have any sexy dreams. I think I'm all sexed out…that is until I wake in the middle of the night ready and raring to go again…poor Branson.

♡

CHAPTER 14

THE NEXT MORNING, I WAKE BEFORE BRANSON. I STRETCH and moan, my body aches all over, but I have never felt so invigorated in my entire life. Resting my head on my hand, I watch him sleep for a few moments. Suddenly, I need to pee—joys of pregnancy—and climb out of bed. After using the bathroom, I slip on my panties and his shirt from yesterday and head to the kitchen. Leaving him to sleep a while longer, after all I did ride him hard in the middle of the night…if the chaffing between my thighs is anything to go by.

After turning the coffee maker on, I lean on the counter and stare out the window and grin. I haven't been this happy in months. My happy moment is interrupted when two hands wrap around my waist, resting on my bump.

Branson nuzzles my ear. "Morning," he says, his hot breath on my neck causing my body to shiver.

Spinning around to face him, I drape my arms over his shoulder. "Morning," I reply, with a super big smile on my face. He lowers his lips to mine and kisses me good morning, his tongue sliding against mine. "Feel free to kiss me like that each and every morning," I say, rubbing my nose against his.

"Duly noted," he says with a nod, his hands slide down my back and my hands grip his naked, taut sexy ass and I squeeze. He returns the squeeze and pulls me closer to him. Slamming his mouth against mine, he kisses me deeply once more. His cock thickens between us, as I circle my hips against his. Before I have time to register what's happening, he spins me around, bends me gently over the kitchen counter edge, lifts his shirt up, tears my panties off me, and slams his cock into me from behind. I start to laugh, he pauses mid-thrust "Why are you laughing?"

Looking over my shoulder at him, I grin. "I dreamt about this exact moment a few weeks ago," I say with a laugh.

"Well, let's see if I can make it better than you dream." Before I can process what he said, he pulls out, spins me around, lifts me up, and sits me on the countertop. He pulls me to the edge and slams back into me. Leaning back on my arms, I wrap my ankles around his hips and pull him closer. He increases his thrusts, bending down; he sucks my nipple through his shirt. He nips the bud, and I crash over the edge. "Braaaaaaaansooooon!" I scream, as my orgasm tears through my body. He soon follows with a guttural growl.

He pulls out, lowers me to my feet and stares at me. "I

can't believe this is finally happening. I've been enamored with you since the first day I met you back in 2009."

"What?" I say, shocked at his words.

"The day you and Kody met and hooked up, I saw you when you and Chloe first walked into the bar, but Kody got to you first. I'd never seen him so smitten, so happy before, so I kept my feelings to myself."

"Wow, I did not know that." Staring at him, I wonder how life would have been different if we hooked up back then. "You really are a fantastic person, Branson Holmes." Wrapping my arms around his shoulders, I place my lips against his. Pulling back I purse my lips.

"What's wrong?"

"How is everyone going to take this?"

"What do you mean?"

"Well, Kody was my fiancé. He's your brother. I'm having his baby, and now you and I are a thing." He grins at me and it warms my heart in a way I never thought possible. "What?"

"You and I are a thing...Never thought that would happen."

Pursing my lips again, I frown. "What's everyone going to think?"

"Who gives a shit what they think?"

"Branson—"

"No," he shakes his head, "I don't give a flying fuck what anyone thinks. You are happy. I'm over the fucking moon happy. Hell, we have Kody's blessing. His blessing is all that matters in my eyes."

"Okay...can we keep it just between us, for now? I want to be in this happy bubble for just a little while longer."

Before he can answer, there's a knock at the door. I look down at what I'm wearing and grimace.

"You go change and I'll answer the door."

Nodding my head, I walk down the hallway, happier than I have been in a longtime. When I turn back to remind him that he's naked, I see that he's slipped on a pair of pants and a shirt from the laundry basket sitting on the table.

Ten minutes later, I emerge and I see Helen and Randall sitting at the island counter chatting with Branson. I see Branson's letter from Kody sitting on the countertop, and I know he's told them what we discovered.

He must sense my presence because he looks up at me. The look on his face confirms my thoughts about them having read the letter. I'm not sure how I feel about that. I was hoping to keep things between us for now, but I guess Kody is their son. They have a right to know, and I can't control what Branson does with his letter.

"Hey, guys," I say, walking over to them.

Both Helen and Randall look toward me. They both smile, and as always lately, their eyes drop to my belly. "Look at you, you're glowing," Helen coos, as she stands up and walks over to me. Enveloping me in a hug before placing her hands on my belly. "Hey, Peanut. Nanny can't wait to meet you."

Peanut decides to kick at that precise moment and Helen's face breaks out into the biggest nanny smile I have ever seen. I find myself smiling at seeing the joy on her face. Then I look up and see Branson staring at me, as usual when I see him looking at me, my heart rate accelerates and happiness courses through my veins. I feel guilty all of a sudden, but when he winks at me, all the anguish I just felt disappears.

Helen sees the wink and she takes my hand in hers and squeezes tightly. Looking to her, she's grinning back at me —when she winks back at me—I know she knows.

"You know, don't you?" I murmur, nerves racing through me with how she's going to react.

She nods at me. "I've had my suspicions for a while but just now, with that wink, they were confirmed."

"I'm sorry," I somberly say.

"What are you sorry about, Kasey?"

"Kody. The baby. Branson. Disappointing you. Everything."

A tear cascades down my cheek, Helen wipes it away, cups my cheeks in that loving mom way, and stares at me. "There is nothing to be sorry about." She pauses and looks to the kitchen. "Branson, make tea for everyone and then come join us in the living room."

Helen drags me into the room. We take a seat on the sofa and Randall sits in the recliner. Helen takes my hand in hers again. "Kasey, the first time I met you, you and Branson were goofing around when Randall and I walked in. I thought in that moment Branson had a new girlfriend, that *you* were a couple." She places emphasis on you. "I was shocked when Kody introduced you to us as his girlfriend." We both go silent, remembering that day. "Kasey, there's always been a connection between you and Branson. So it's not surprising at all that you two are now together."

I'm stunned at her reply. "But what about Kody?"

"What about him?" she nonchalantly replies.

"He was my fiancé. He's the father of this little one," I say rubbing my belly, "What about all that?"

"What about it? No one can control love, just go with it. Everyone deserves love, Kasey."

"Kody used to say that all the time." I smile as I remember him saying this to Gage last year.

"He got it from me, my boy did listen to me after all." We both laugh. "The heart wants what the heart wants, Kasey. Just go with it." She pauses and looks at me, with a smile, she adds, "Ask yourself this, are you happy with Branson?"

Nodding my head, I whisper, "Yes."

"And did Kody not write two letters saying it was okay to move on? Okay to be happy?" Again I nod my head. "Then go for it. Make my son as happy as you made his brother."

"Ohh, Helen," I cry, tears pouring down my cheeks, again. "I'm sorry, I'm so emotional at the moment. Anything and everything sets the waterworks off. I was so worried you'd think I was a whore and not be happy for us. It's been playing on my mind ever since I realized I had feelings for him. At first, I thought it was just pregnancy hormones, but then we found the letters and we both gave in." I sniff, "Branson told me you'd be okay with it all. I should have trusted him."

"Sweetie, I have eyes. I've seen this coming for the last few months. Even Randall noticed."

"Really?" I scoff.

"Yes, dear. Even I saw this coming and I'm a man," Randall adds with a laugh.

"We were just waiting for you two to catch up," Helen confirms.

"I can't believe this. I was worried the happy bubble Branson and I have been in was going to pop, but you and Randall have put everything I was worried about at ease. Thank you for understanding. Now I just need to tell my parents."

Helen laughs, "Pretty sure they know too. It seems, everyone but you and Branson knew."

"I guess so," I reply, my eyes drift again to Branson and I find myself smiling.

"Kasey, when you become a parent, you'll do anything for your children. When we lost Kody, I thought my world was going to crash down around me. Then you told us you were pregnant, I knew all was going to be right in the world." She wipes a stray tear away. "And then you fell in love with Branson, and once again, everything was perfect."

"Ohh, Helen," I cry again. She wraps her arms around me when I feel Branson sit next to me. Turning to him, I nuzzle into his side and cry happy tears. "I'm sooo happy," I sob.

The three of them laugh at me.

Branson pulls me tighter into his side and kisses the side of my head. After the last tear has fallen, I pull back and gaze at him. "I love you," I whisper.

"Love you too," he says, as he places a kiss on the top of my nose.

With a smile, I lean back into the couch and rub my belly. This will be okay after all. There is nothing to worry about. Everything will be fine.

CHAPTER 15

...December 7th, 2019

THE LAST FEW WEEKS HAVE PASSED BY IN A BLUR. AS HELEN assured me, Mom and Dad were more than okay with this new development in my love life. They were thrilled to see their baby girl smiling and happy again. And I am, I'm the happiest I have been since losing Kody.

Branson and I are now officially a couple, we made it public knowledge at the surprise baby shower Stacey and Branson threw for me at Bin 501. Much to my surprise, there were no ill feelings toward our pairing. Most people had the same assumption as Helen; when they first met us all, they thought that Branson and I were together, not Kody and I. That notion upsets me a little because I loved Kody with everything I had, but as Branson keeps reminding me, 'its doesn't matter what anyone else thinks or assumes.'

It's easy to say that, but I don't want my actions to tarnish the memory of Kody. Again, Branson assures me that's not the case, and Kody could tarnish his own reputation without anyone's assistance. I laugh when he says this to me, but it's true, Kody marched to the beat of his own drum and that's what I loved most about him. His 'I don't give a shit what anyone thinks' attitude.

Peanut is now due in three weeks, the pregnancy has flown by but at the same time, it's passed really really slowly. My belly is huge, my toes are no longer visible to me—even when I lean forward—but my sex drive has gone into overdrive and skyrocketed; poor Branson. He hasn't complained…yet…but I'm pretty confident he'd like a reprieve.

Lucky for him the last couple of days have been crazy busy with the final preparations for the charity toy drive. I'm really excited for this year's event. We are much more organized than last year. Once again, Marlee, Chelle, and I make a great team AND Gage rocked as our Santa once again.

Even though Chelle is working from home since returning from maternity leave, she's been in most days to assist us. And most days, I get told off for doing too much. Just because I'm the size of a whale doesn't mean I can't organize, or assist with the toy drive.

Today is toy drive day and just like last year, it's go… go…go. Then I'll have my last week of work and come the fourteenth, I'll officially be on maternity leave.

"Ready to rock?" Looking up, I see Marlee standing in my doorway; she's glowing and smiling at me.

"Yep. I just need to grab—"

"Already got them from the break room." She holds up my snow peas and salsa. "I seriously don't know how you can eat this concoction. It's disgusting."

Ungracefully, I stand up and waddle over to her. She's one of few people in this office who doesn't laugh at me; her fiancé is the worst of them all. We link arms, step out of my office, and we bump into Gage. His face lights up when he sees Marlee, much like hers does.

It's so nice to see Gage happy and content.

"What up, Buttercup?" he says to me when he finally notices my presence.

"What have a told you about calling me Buttercup?"

He shrugs his shoulders at me then winks before placing a hand gently on my bump. "Hey, Peanut." He's done this every day since my belly exploded in size. He's one of the many people who supported Branson and I being together. There were a few sly comments and sniggers, but all in all, everyone was very supportive of our budding relationship. Since we gave in to our desires, I've been much more relaxed and happy. I never realized I was putting pressure on myself, but as soon as Branson and I gave in and accepted what was between us, my blood pressure leveled out and life, in general, became much easier for me. For us.

We round the corner into reception, and I smile when I see Branson standing at the front desk chatting to Stacey. He's wearing a Santa hat on his head, jeans that hug his ass perfectly, and a navy blue button-down shirt with the sleeves rolled to his elbows. He's the definition of 'smoking hot' right now.

He must sense my presence because he looks over to

me and grins. His smile lights up his face and sets my panties on fire.

Marlee turns to Gage and not so quietly whispers, "Holy shit, with that one look the temperature in here just rose a billion degrees."

"Even I can feel it, and I'm a dude," Gage confirms.

My eyes are locked on Branson; I didn't even realize that Chelle is now standing next to me. It isn't until she taps me on the arm that I register her presence. "Huh?"

"I said, are you ready to go?"

"What?" I ask again, completely confused right now. All I can think about is the throb between my thighs and how fucking sexy Branson looks right now.

"Friggin' hell," Chelle scoffs, as she snaps her fingers in my face. 'Focus. Toy drive day."

Nodding my head, I mumble, "Yep...Sex drive...I mean toy drive."

Chelle shakes her head and drags me toward the elevator. "Let's go, whore."

"I'm not a whore, I'm just horny and pregnant."

"My apologies," Chelle says, before adding, "you are a pregnant whore."

My eyes snap to hers and she's staring at me with a 'don't-try-and-deny-it' look on her face. Shrugging my shoulders, I say, "Yeah. I got nothing."

Branson walks up behind me and wraps his arms around me, gently caressing my belly. He kisses my ear. "Hey, sexy lady."

"Hey," I say, turning my head to look at him before I sneak a quick kiss.

"Get a room, you two," Gage says, just as the elevator doors open.

"How about an elevator instead?" Branson says.

I giggle. Gage scoffs. Chelle says, "Hell no. Get the next one, Holmes."

We all laugh and step into the car. Before the doors even close, Chelle whips out her folder and as the elevator goes down, she reads through her list, reminding everyone of our jobs when we get there. She looks at me, points, and snarls, "Don't even think about lifting anything heavy or awkward or anything bigger than a pen. If I had it my way, we'd have left you behind, but I don't want preg-zilla to rear her ugly head on what's going to be a joyous afternoon. So do as your told, and I'll be sure to put in a good word with the big man in red."

Without batting an eyelid, I raise my hand to my temple and salute her, "Sir, yes, sir."

Everyone laughs and as I look around the car, I know it's going to be a great day.

Just as I predicted, the afternoon was a success and the kids all had a wonderful time. Seeing the look of joy on all their faces makes this all worth it. And once again, Gage was a fabulous Santa.

Overhearing a conversation between him and Marlee gave me an idea for tonight, and I cannot wait to surprise Branson when he gets home. Now I'm glad he was called into the bar for an emergency, because it gives me time to race home and set up my Christmas surprise.

♡

CHAPTER 16

AFTER SAYING GOODBYE TO EVERYONE WHEN WE RETURNED TO the office, I made my way as fast as my fat ass would allow to my car and I drove home. Glancing in the back, when I place my handbag on the front seat, I smile when I see Peanut's car seat already installed.

Branson, the ever-awesome man that he is, has already installed one in my car, one in his car, and has one sitting in my garage for his mom's car. My mom already has her own, I cannot believe how overboard everyone is going with baby stuff. The nursery at home is about to explode.

Not that I've told anyone, but I'm going to donate some of the baby stuff to charity. There's so much and Peanut doesn't need all of this, and neither do I.

Traffic is light and I make it home in record time.

Racing inside, I head straight to the bedroom. I open my drawer, pull out what I'm looking for, and head into the bathroom. Stepping under the hot water, I moan when the droplets hit my skin. The pressure is amazing and I can feel the tension washing away.

Quickly, I jump out and dry myself. Just as I step into the bedroom, my phone pings with a text.

BRANSON: *Just leaving now. Need anything?*
KASEY: *Nope, just you home. I'm in bed reading. See you soon Xo*
BRANSON: *Quiet nite snuggling sounds awesome Xo*

Grinning when I read his last message, I slip on my black G-sting and walk back into the bathroom to fix my hair. Once all the flyaways have been straightened, I slap on some lip gloss and head back into the bedroom.

Grabbing my Santa hat, I lay across the bottom of the bed, with my ass to the door and lean my head on my hand. Just as I've gotten comfortable, I hear Branson pull into the driveway and I grin. "It's showtime."

Picking up the hat, I place it on my hip, and hold it up, trying to get the hat to stand up but it keeps flopping down. I hear Branson coming toward the bedroom. My heart rate increases, I'm nervous. I'm excited and I'm scared. This is the first time I have ever done anything sexy like this, and I just hope that in my current state, I don't look like a beached whale.

Closing my eyes, I smile when I hear Branson gasp. Even though my back is to him, I can feel his gaze roaming over my body. Twisting my neck, I glance over my shoulder at him and wink. "Merry Christmas."

"Merry Christmas indeed." He pauses. "Babe, you are the sexiest present I have ever received."

In two steps, he's at the edge of the bed. He runs his finger up my calf—goosebumps appear on my skin—he traces his finger up my thigh and over my ass cheek. A giggle slips from my lip, *so romantic*, I think, but that thought soon disappears when I feel his lips kissing my bare shoulder. My head drops back and then his lips are on mine.

Closing my eyes, my mouth opens slightly and his tongue slides in. Dropping the Santa hat, I run my fingers through his hair, pulling him into the kiss. Rolling over to face him, which I manage to do in a sexy...ish way. Branson pulls me into a sitting position, places his palms face down on the mattress, and kisses me again. This kiss is hungrier than the last.

With our lips fused together, I lift my hands and unbuckle his belt, flick open the button, lower his fly, and slide my hands in, pulling his briefs and jeans down in one fluid motion. Without breaking our kiss, he kicks his pants to the side.

Standing up, he cups my cheeks and stares down at me. Never have I felt more alive than I do in this moment. Sliding off the edge of the bed to my knees, I stare up at him as I grab his cock and bring it to my lips. Kissing the tip, I open my mouth and suck. Branson groans as I continue to slide his dick in and out of my mouth.

He grabs under my shoulders and lifts me to my feet, slamming his lips against mine for a searing hot kiss. He gently lowers me to the mattress; normally he'd cocoon my body with his, but due to my belly that isn't possible at the moment. He pulls his shirt over his head and lies on the bed next to me. We face each other and kiss like teenagers. My lips are raw from kissing, but I want more. I always want more when it comes to Branson.

Shuffling to my knees, I carefully climb over Branson and lower myself onto him. We both moan as I rock back and forth. Resting my hands on his chest for balance, he covers my hands with his and we entwine our fingers together. He lifts our joined hands and together we massage and play with my breasts. My nipples are very tender and I flinch, a quiet, "Ouch," slips from my lips, but I slide our hands down my body to my clit.

Together we rub and circle my clit, that's what I need to send me soaring, and I crash over the orgasmic edge, my body shudders as pleasure courses through my veins. My body tingles in the most delicious way from head to toe. My shudders have just stopped when I feel Branson's body tense beneath me and his orgasm releases inside of me.

Rolling off him, I lie down and stare at the ceiling. My breathing hurried from my super intense orgasm. Branson grabs my hand and brings it to his lips, kissing my knuckles. Turning my head to face him, he murmurs, "I love you, Kasey Wellson."

Leaning over, I kiss his shoulder. "I love you, too."

With a smile on my face, and my hand laced with Branson's on my bump, I happily drift off to sleep with the man I love soundly snoring beside me. I'm the happiest I've been in months, and nothing will change that.

♡

CHAPTER 17

…December 13th, 2019

"WE CANNOT WAIT TO MEET BABY WELLSON, AND WE WISH you and Branson all the very best," Gage says to everyone who's squeezed into the conference room. Everyone claps and cheers and then goes back to their conversations and the food. Oh my God, the food, there's sooo much. The conference table is full. There's cake, sushi—totally mean to have this around a pregnant lady—hot and cold platters, and did I mention cake? And directly in front of me is the biggest plate of snow pea and salsa. This is the perfect send-off.

Tomorrow is my first day of maternity leave. I'm excited but also a little sad. I've worked here for the past four years, it will be odd not coming in each day but the adventure ahead is pretty awesome. Peanut gives me a little—okay—massive kick, and I take that to mean she's pretty excited too. I cannot wait to meet him, or hold her in my arms; gaze into her eyes that I hope are just like her daddy's, and I'll be sure to tell her stories about Kody every day. My eyes well with tears when I think about him and all that he'll miss.

Walking to the side of the conference room, I take a seat and rest my hand on my belly; the emotion of everything catching up to me.

"You okay?" Gage asks, as he sits next to me, grabbing my hand and squeezing it reassuringly.

Nodding my head, "Yes. No. I don't know." The first tear falls. "Gage, I miss Kody so much right now. He would have made the best father."

"And you'll make the best mother," he says, as he pulls me into a side hug. Resting my head on his shoulder, I let the tears fall. "Why did this have to happen?" I blubber.

"So you and Branson could fall in love. Kismet is a bitch, Buttercup. At times she works in mysterious ways, but there's always a reason for it. I think in this case, Kody's passing is what bought you and Branson together. If you had hooked up with him instead of Kody, who knows what path your life would have taken?" He pauses. "Ask yourself this, are you happy with Branson?" I nod my head. "Then that's all that matters. Sure, it sucks Kody isn't here, but he still is," he rests his hand on my belly, "in the form of this little munchkin."

Wiping my eyes, I look to Gage. "When did you get so wise and shit?"

"Just over twelve months ago, when I crashed into the love of my life."

Smiling, I shake my head. "Never in my wildest dreams did I ever think Gage Grainger would fall in love."

"Kody knew."

"Yeah, he did, didn't he? He was a pretty wise man, and I guess he knew he wasn't going to be around forever either. His letters prove that."

"See, kismet."

"Yes, kismet." I pause and subconsciously start rubbing my belly.

Once again, Gage covers my hands. "Kase, you are going to be fine. Trust me."

"You once told me never to trust anyone who says 'trust me,' especially if it was you."

"I lied."

We both laugh.

"Dude, I'm going to miss seeing your ugly face every day."

"And I'll miss your bitchiness."

"I'm not a bitch," I scoff, playfully whacking him in the arm.

"I know, you are THE bitch." He quickly jumps up before I can hit him again.

He leans down and places a kiss on my head. "You've got this, Buttercup." He walks off and leaves me sitting here smiling. I don't know how Gage does it, but he always manages to put me and my mind at ease.

The party wraps up and I head back to my office. Walking over to my desk, I sit down, lean back, and look around the room. Memories of the last four years come flooding back to me, and once again I tear up; damn freakin' hormones.

After my pity party, I close the door and walk over to my couch. I'll lie down for ten minutes for a rest, and then

I'll tidy up my desk and head home. I'm pretty sure I'm asleep before I even lift my feet off the floor.

When I wake up, I'm a little disorientated. Blinking a few times, I realize I'm in my office. Standing up, I walk over to my desk and flick on the lamp, but as soon as the light pops on, the bulb blows and the room is shrouded in darkness once again. Grabbing my phone, I turn on the flashlight and see that it's 8:00 p.m. and I have three missed calls from Branson. "Damn, I must have really been out."

Pulling up my contacts, I dial Branson as I walk over toward the door and flick the overhead lights on. He picks up on the second ring as I'm squinting from the blinding light.

"Kasey, babe, where are you? Are you all right?"

"I'm fine. I'm still at the office. I laid down for a quick nap but my quick nap turned into a five-hour sleep. Sorry to worry you."

"I wasn't worried."

"Liar."

"Okay, I was a little worried, but I knew if something was wrong you'd call."

"I'm sorry. I think I'll just come home now and come back tomorrow to finish up."

"Babe, it's a total whiteout at the moment. You're better off staying there until it passes."

Just as he says this, the power goes out. "Shit."

"What's wrong? Is it Peanut?"

"You always think it's Peanut. She is fine. It's the power, it just went out."

Just as I say this, a sharp cramping pain shoots through my stomach, I lean forward, rest my hand on the desk, and breathe deeply. I'm still holding the phone to my ear but

I'm not registering anything Branson is saying. The cramping in my stomach is getting stronger and stronger as the moments pass, then the worst possible thing happens, "Fuuuuuck!" I groan.

"What's wrong?" Branson says, his voice full of concern.

"My water just broke."

CHAPTER 18

"What do you mean your water broke? You aren't due until the twenty-seventh?"

"I mean, I'm standing in a puddle of water right now and my stomach is tight and…" Tears well in my eyes. "Branson, she's coming. I can feel it."

"Don't panic, I'm on my way."

"Branson, please don't leave me. Stay on the…fuuuuuuuck…line."

"I'm here and I'm not going anywhere." In the background I can hear the car start and the engine rumbles as he starts to drive. "Shit, it's really coming down now."

"Branson, please be safe. I need you. I can't do this alone," I cry.

"I'm coming, babe, I'll be there in twenty minutes."

Another contraction tears through me, then another, each one stronger and stronger. "Branson, I need you."

"I'm coming. I'll be there soon. You are the strongest person I know. You can do this. Just focus on your breathing."

Closing my eyes, I listen to Branson and concentrate on my breathing. The next contraction hits, but it's not as bad as the previous ones when I focus on my breathing. My eyes pop open, "It's worked. That one wasn't half as bad." Just as I finish saying that, another one tears through me. "Fuuuuuuuck." Through the phone I can hear Branson repeating, 'Breathe, just breathe,' over and over.

"Shut the fuck up with the breathing crap. I know how to fucking breathe!" I scream. Then I quickly add, "I'm sorry, I'm sooo sorry. How far away are you? I need you here, Branson. Please."

"Not far, I promise. Kase, I'm going to hang up, call the paramedics, and then I'll call you right back."

"No, please don't leave me," I whine.

"Babe, you need a paramedic. I'll be back on the line as quick as I can. I love you."

"I love you too," I say, but all I hear is the beeping of him hanging up.

Sliding to the floor, leaning against my bookshelf, I begin to cry, wondering if this is the punishment for falling in love with Branson. That thought evaporates as soon as my phone starts ringing again. When I answer, I put it on speaker this time. "Branson, I love you and I'm sorry I was a cow."

"Hello to you too." We both laugh. "Kase, I love you more than you love snow peas and salsa."

"So lots then?"

"Very much so. You'll be pleased to know the paramedics are on their way, and I have just pulled up and I'm about to walk inside. Now since the power's out, I'm going to have to take the stairs. Service will drop out, but I will be there as soon as I can."

"Okay, hurry."

He hangs up and another contraction hits, this one was quicker and sharper than the last few. From what I've read, I'm pretty sure this baby is going to come any moment now. Leaning my head back, I close my eyes and focus on my breathing—in though my nose, out through my mouth. I'm really hoping this will slow things down, but as with everything in my life, that isn't the case. Another contraction, the strongest so far, hits and I groan out in pain.

My office door bangs open, and I look up to see Branson standing in the doorway. "I'm here," he says, as he falls to his knees and places a kiss on my forehead.

"Branson, I need to push," I grunt through clenched teeth.

Branson goes into baby delivery mode. He pulls off my panties, rearranges me so I'm lying down on a couch cushion, but also in a semi-sitting position. He spreads my legs and his mouth drops open. "Fuck, I can see the head."

He squeezes my knees. "Kase, look at me." Looking up at him, we smile at each other. "Okay, on the next contraction I want you to push."

Nodding my head, I swallow deeply. "Now." I moan and with all my might I push and push with the contraction. Letting out the breath I was holding when it passes, I begin to breathe normally again.

Branson says, "On the next one, another super big push."

My head nods on its own accord. My eyes are focused

on Branson, while he is concentrating hard on my vagina right now, which hurts like nothing I have ever felt before. The contraction begins and I clench my teeth and push. "Arrrrrrrrrgh." My muscles tense and then all of a sudden, the room is quiet, and then the most magical sound I have ever heard erupts. Baby Holmes wails; it's an amazing sound. My eyes well with tears and Branson says, "It's a boy."

Immediately I think of Kody, this moment is happy yet sad at the same time. All those sad thoughts evaporate when, after wrapping him in a blanket off the couch, Branson hands him to me. Gazing down at my baby boy, the tears break free and through an avalanche of tears, I kiss my little man on his forehead. "Hey, baby boy. I'm your mommy."

Branson sits down next to us, wraps his arm around me, and I snuggle into his side. He has his phone to his ear, from the end of the conversation I can hear, he's talking to the paramedics again. He hangs up and then kisses my temple. "You did good, Mommy. He's...I have no words."

"This here is your daddy, little man." I look up at Branson and smile. "He loves you just as much as I do."

We both silently stare as he suckles away at my breast.

Glancing back up at Branson, I lean forward when he looks at me and we kiss. The moment is broken when from out in the hallway we hear someone yell, "Hello!"

"Down here!" Branson shouts back, his eyes still on mine. A few moments later, we hear shuffling coming down the hallway. "In here, guys!" Branson yells again, startling the baby and he begins to cry.

"Shhhh," I whisper as I gently tap his bottom to settle him.

Two paramedics enter and they both smile. "Well, look at that, a beautiful family."

A smile breaks free and I look up at them. "Yes, Kody here decided he couldn't wait."

"Kody?" Branson questions.

"Yep, Kody Gage Holmes," I say, placing a kiss on his head before looking up at Branson. His face is void of any emotion, and then I wonder if maybe I should have said something to him about the name first, but my anguish is eased when he smiles and whispers, "It's perfect."

CHAPTER 19

I'VE JUST DOZED OFF TO SLEEP WHEN THERE'S A KNOCK AT MY hospital room door, opening my eyes; the door opens and in walks Mom and Dad.

"Hey, Pumpkin," Dad says, as he walks over to me and places kiss on my forehead. Mom makes a beeline for the bassinet and Kody. She clutches her chest and looks over at me. "He's gorgeous, Kase." She notices his name on the card and she covers her mouth and scoffs.

"What is it, Trudy?" Dad asks Mom.

"His…his name. It's…it's perfect. Kasey, I love it."

"What's his name?" Dad asks.

"Kody Gage Holmes," Mom replies before I get a chance.

"Kase, that's beautiful. I thought Branson would be here, especially after the events of last night."

"I sent him home to shower and bring back everything I need."

Dad nods as he walks over to Mom. They both gaze lovingly down at Kody and as I watch them, that happy-sad feeling crashes into me. A sob breaks free. Mom looks at me, and her mom instinct kicks in because I know she realizes what I'm feeling. She walks over to me; her arms wide open for a hug. She envelops me in a mom hug, and I cry. I cry that Kody isn't here to enjoy this with me. And I cry for feeling like this in regard to Branson.

Mom whispers into my ear, "You are allowed to be sad but don't dwell, Kody wouldn't want that. He would want you, Kody, and Branson to be happy and to live life to the fullest."

"You sound like Helen," I sniff.

"Us moms know all. Welcome to the club, baby girl." That makes me laugh.

Pulling back from Mom, I wipe my eyes. "Thanks, Mom."

"Anytime, Kase. Anytime."

Kody cries from his bassinet, and Dad sheepishly says, "I better pick him up." He leans down and as he carefully picks Kody up, he says, in that baby voice, "I'm your grumpy, KJ." He coos, "That lady there," he points to Mom, "is your Nana. And you've already met your mom and Bra...Dad. You are one lucky little dude but just remember, I'm the coolest one of them all."

I laugh at that part and then I click that he called Kody, KJ. "Dad, KJ?" I question.

"Kody Junior, or KJ," Dad says, as he takes a seat and

turns into a big soft teddy bear as he cradles his grandson in his arms.

"KJ, I like it," I say as Mom and I watch him fuss over Kody. I didn't think my heart could be so full of love, until Branson comes in bearing a tray of coffee, a cute teddy bear, and a gorgeous bouquet of blue chrysanthemums, my favorite. Followed by Helen and Randall, who make a beeline to Dad and the three of them goo and gah over Kody, or KJ, as Dad now affectionately calls him.

"Hey, you," I happily say, as Branson walks over to me. He places the coffees on the tray table, the teddy on the end of the bed, and Mom takes the flowers from him; telling us she'll grab a vase to pop them in. He places a kiss on my forehead and I get a whiff of his aftershave. Closing my eyes, I breathe him in and smile.

"Hey," he says when he pulls back.

We stare intently at one another. We haven't had a moment alone together since Kody arrived last night. I was worried it would be awkward, but it's not. It's exactly how things were before and I'm over the moon happy about that. He takes a seat on the bed and hands me a coffee. "How you feeling?"

"Dying for a coffee and a shower."

"I've ticked one of those things off your list." He stares intently at me and adds, "I'm happy to help with option two." He raises his eyebrows suggestively at me and I laugh.

"Ease up, cowboy. I just pushed a human-shaped watermelon out my va-jay-jay. I'm stretched beyond anything I thought possible down there, and in no way do I feel sexy right now. You need to wait...like six to ten years."

Branson laughs but when he sees the serious look on

my face he immediately stops. "Okay, no hanky panky, but I'm happy to help you shower."

"Do you promise not to cop a feel?"

"Can't promise that because, babe, your tits look fucking spectacular right now."

A clearing throat from behind us causes us to look over to Dad, who has a stern look on his face, but at the same time he's trying to hide his grin.

"Sorry, Dad, totally forgot you were still here," I say.

"Clearly," he says. "But you've given me this little cutie-patootie, so I'll allow your watermelon vagina comment to pass."

"Dad!" I scoff. "Don't ever say that again."

"I won't if you won't," he playfully replies. Kody starts getting antsy in his arms. "I think someone's hungry again. But first, Branson, you need to change his diaper."

Dad winks at me and I look inquisitively at him. Branson hops up, takes Kody from him, and walks over to the changing table. He's getting everything ready while keeping an eye on Kody lying there. He removes Kody's diaper and his eyes bug open. "Oh my God!"

Immediately, I jump out of bed, flinching at the sudden movements. I'm next to Brandon is no time and when I look down, I gag. "Eeeeew, gross. What the hell is that?"

Dad's pissing himself laughing right now, just as Mom walks in. "What's so funny?" She looks to me. "Kase, what's wrong?"

"That," I say, pointing to Kody's diaper. Mom steps over and she starts laughing, just like Dad.

"That's just meconium. Totally normal."

"Black tar like shit is normal?"

Mom nods. "Yep, the first few will be like that."

"That's just wrong." I shudder and walk back over to the bed.

"At least you aren't cleaning it up."

Dad is still laughing his ass off. "You do realize that Branson is going to get you back for that."

"Maybe he'll get a number three," Mom jokes.

Branson snaps his head around. "A number three? Do I even want to know?"

Mom shakes her head. "Nope. And now I pray that your father gets it. Sorry, Steve."

"Bring it on." Dad says, his voice laced with fear.

"But seriously," I ask, "what's a number three?"

"There are no words to describe a number three. Just hope and pray, you are not the one to get it."

Branson finishes changing the black poopy diaper from hell and passes Kody to me. Once again he latches on to my breast and begins to suckle. As he drinks, I sit and stare at him; amazed that Kody and I created this tiny little human being, who for the last nine months grew in my belly. And now, he's here: the last piece of Kody, my eyes well with tears.

Branson, places his hand on my knee. "He'd be so proud of you."

Looking up, I swallow the lump in my throat. "How did you know I was thinking about him?"

"You get this melancholic look on your face when you do."

"I'm sorry," I whisper, as a tear drops over the edge and streaks down my cheek, landing on Kody's head.

"Don't you ever apologize for thinking about him. He was a huge part of your life, and mine. I never want his memory to fade. I want Kody here to know that his dad was the best man ever."

"You are his dad too," I say, "Kody here is lucky to have two amazing dads." Reaching over, I grab Branson's hand and bring it to my lips, placing a kiss on his knuckles. "I love you, Branson."

"I love you too," he says, leaning forward, he grips my cheeks and gently places his lips against mine. Closing my eyes, I give myself over to the kiss and know that Branson, KJ, and I will be fine.

CHAPTER 20

"Why, KJ, why? Why do you like to be awake at stupid o'clock?" I whine, as I sit in the glider rocker, trying to get KJ to sleep. It's stupid o'clock in the morning, and I feel like a complete zombie. Chelle told me nighttimes can be tough, but my golly gosh—new language since the arrival of KJ—it's much tougher than I thought.

We've been home from hospital for three nights now, and KJ thinks nighttime is party time, and by party time I mean he cries for hours on end. Branson is a godsend, but as he doesn't have boobs and milk, it's all on me...and I wouldn't have it any other way. Sure, I'd like some more sleep, but KJ is perfect in every way possible.

Even though he arrived a few weeks early, everything with him was perfect. As the nurse said, "Imagine if he went full term?" That would have been almost two extra weeks of growth and pushing him out at his size of nine pounds one ounce was tough enough.

Finally he has fallen asleep but I'm too exhausted myself to move, so I close my eyes and drift off to sleep in the chair with Kody in my arms.

Waking the next morning, I look down at the bundle of joy in my arms and I smile, he's still sound asleep, quietly snoring. Seeing his cute lil' chubby face all relaxed and asleep is the best way to wake up. Looking up, I see Branson standing in the doorway staring lovingly at us. He's shirtless and only wearing a pair of low sitting boxers. My insides tingle but at the same time cringe… how can I crave sex, but at the same time shudder at the thought of a penis going anywhere near my hoo-ha?

"Morning, gorgeous," he says, as he steps into the room and over to us. He places a kiss on my forehead and smiles at me. Again, that smile zaps through me and I find myself grinning back. Branson notices the tinge to my cheeks and raises his eyebrows at me. Shaking my head, I pull a 'no-way-in-hell' face. He laughs, causing Kody to wake in my arms.

He opens his dark, chocolate brown eyes, just like his daddy's, and goos at us. Branson lifts him from my arms. "Morning, little man. You really need to learn that night-time is for sleeping." He kisses his chubby cheeks and walks over to the changing table and changes his diaper. I take the reprieve to head to the bathroom to freshen up.

When I come back, the two of them are in the glider and Branson is telling him a story about him and Kody when they were younger. My eyes well with tears as I watch the two of them; it becomes too much and I race into our bedroom and collapse onto the bed and sob. A few moments later the bed dips, rolling over I see Branson staring down at me, his face etched with worry. "Are you okay?" he asks, brushing a strand of hair off my face.

"Yes. No. I don't know," I sniff, "Hearing you talk about him with…" I sob again, "with Kody just tears at my heart, but at the same time it makes me happy, knowing he'll know Kody even though he isn't here." By now I'm sobbing uncontrollably. Branson pulls me into his arms and hugs me, rubbing my back, whispering sweet nothings into my ear.

He pulls back at stares at me, his face stern. "Do not ever feel bad for crying over losing Kody. We all miss him. I want that little boy to know who his biological dad is, I will never take that from him, or you."

"Ohh, Branson," I sob once again.

We hear Kody fussing though the monitor. "I better go feed him."

"No, stay here. I'll bring him to you."

A few moments later, they come back in and Branson hands Kody to me. The three of us settle on the bed. I feed Kody and Branson and I chat, the three of us a perfect, happy little family. Watching Branson while I feed Kody, my heart soars. In that moment, I make a decision that will change our future…I just hope Branson agrees and says yes.

CHAPTER 21

...December 31st, 2019

Our first Christmas with Kody was low-key and quiet, in other words it was perfect. Mom, Dad, Helen, and Randall came over and we had a lovely day together. Mom and Helen cooked an amazing meal, and I was banished from my own kitchen. Because I'm breastfeeding, I couldn't even indulge in Randall's eggnog, which is the best. I was told, however, I could have a glass on New Year's Eve...if I was a good girl. Ha, fat chance of that happening but with what I have in mind, I WILL be having a glass on New Year's.

All week I've been telling Branson we will be going to

Bin 501 for New Year's Eve, he complains and says no, but I put my foot down. We have been cooped at home since Kody was born, we venture to the store or out for a walk only. We deserve a night out, a night to let our hair down. Finally he relents and agrees…but no matter what he said, it was happening.

Earlier in the day, with help from Gage and Marlee, whom I suspect is pregnant, they help us set up a Pack 'n Play in Branson's office for Kody, and then we turn the wine bar into THE place to be, to bring in 2020; how is it nearly 2020 already? Marlee keeps asking me if I'm okay, and I reassure her I'm fine, but if I'm honest, I'm a nervous Nelly right now. All different what-if scenarios flit through my mind, but I push the worry aside and forge ahead with my plan.

We arrive at Bin 501 just after 6:00 p.m., later than I wanted to, but we were delayed due to the 'Great poop explosion of 2019!' We finally got the number three that dad talked about, and Oh My Fucking God—yes, I swore —it was the worst shit I have ever dealt with in my life. Who knew someone so small could produce something so vile?

We can laugh now, but at the time—nope—no laughter was had at all.

Of course, as soon as we arrive, Kody is abducted and passed around everyone. No surprise, but Dad ends up with him and the two of them hang out for the rest of the night together. The only time I get to hold my son is when I need to feed him, but as soon I'm finished, he's in Dad's arms again. Who knew my dad was such a softie?

Washing my hands after using the toilet, I stare at my reflection and smile. I was going to wait until midnight, but I can't. I need to do this now before I lose my nerve. Exiting the restrooms, I find Branson by the bar. Walking over to him, I tap him on the shoulder. He spins around to face me and when he realizes it's me, he grins back. "Hey, you." I say, as I slide my arm around his waist.

"Hey, you," he replies, placing a kiss on my forehead.

"Can I borrow you for a moment?"

"Sure, everything okay?" he asks, his voice lace with concern.

Smiling at him, I nod. "Yes, it's perfect."

Lacing our fingers together, I head toward the front entrance and I grab our jackets. "Here put this on and follow me." He doesn't argue and slips his coat on and follows me outside.

The snow is really coming down. I think maybe we should go inside, but Branson wraps his arms around me, and when I feel the warmth radiating from him, I know this is the perfect moment. Wrapping my arms around his waist, I gaze up at him. I take a deep breath, and begin, "Branson, you have been my everything since we lost Kody. What started out as consoling one another turned into something I never imagined. You were with me every step of the pregnancy; hell, you even delivered our son. You are always there for me, and I want to always be there for you. Branson, will you—" before I get to ask him, he drops to his knee and pulls out a gorgeous, square-cut engagement ring with a diamond encrusted in the band.

"Kasey, everything you just said is exactly how I feel. I know you were going to ask me, but it's not happening that way, I'm doing the asking. Will you marry me?"

"I want to say no 'cause you ruined my moment, but yes, yes, I'll marry you."

He slides the ring onto my finger. I wrap my arms around his neck and kiss him with everything I have. "I love you," I whisper against his lips.

"I love you too. Now let's take this inside before we freeze to death."

With all the nerves I had, I hadn't noticed it is now snowing like crazy. He takes my left hand, laces our hands together, kisses my engagement ring, and we head back inside. When the door slams shut behind us, all heads turn to face us. Branson lifts our joined hands and shouts, "She said yes!"

The room erupts into a cheer, my face breaks into a smile, and suddenly everyone encroaches upon us to congratulate us and to get a look at my ring. Which is stunning, he picked well.

It's nearly midnight and our little man is awake again, so I find a quiet corner and feed him. I've just finished feeding him, when Branson comes over. "Here's my two favorite people."

He sits next to me and bends down to place a kiss on Kody's forehead. Kody is passed out in my arms, even with the noise around us, he's sound asleep. The count-down begins and everyone is rowdy and celebrating.

3...

2...

1...

Happy New Year!

Turning to Branson, I whisper, "Happy New Year, fiancé."

"Happy New year, fiancée."

We lean toward each other and bring in the new year with a sensual kiss. Closing my eyes, I lose myself in the perfect first kiss of 2020. Opening my eyes, I see Branson staring at me and his stare penetrates deep into my soul. 2019 was a tough year, but I got through it, mostly due to the man beside me. I'm excited for 2020 and the adventure that awaits us.

EPILOGUE

...December 13th, 2020

"Happy birthday, dear KJ. Happy birthday to you. HIP HIP HOORAY."

We all sing "Happy Birthday" to Kody, he's sitting on Branson's lap in front of his first birthday cake. He's clapping with joy. He looks at me a with a gummy grin and then dives his hand into the cake. Everyone laughs and then he turns to Branson, offering his cake-covered hands to him. And by offer, I mean wiping his hand across Branson's chin, covering it in frosting. Laughter erupts once more and this encourages KJ to do it again. Branson grabs his chubby little wrists and pretends to gobble them. Kody pulls his hands free and proceeds to lick his fingers.

Taking a seat next to them I smile, I can't believe my little man is one already. Leaning toward Branson, I kiss and lick his chin clean. My eyes are locked on his; they have that 'I want to ravage you' glint to them. He leans into me, and whispers, "Later." My insides clench and tingle with what's to come later. My mind drifts to the first time after having KJ…

…It was February 14th, 2019, Valentine's Day, Mom and Dad, now known as Grumpy and Nana, offered to watch him so we could go out to dinner. We dropped him off at their place, and then to my surprise, Branson drove us home again. We pulled into the driveway and he pulled out a blindfold.

"I need you to put this on and trust me."

Without batting an eyelid, I lean over and kiss him passionately before I take the blindfold from him and slip it on. "Let's do this."

Branson laughs but I hear his door open. I sit in the car and wait—my nerves are building. They are a mixture of excitement, arousal, and fear. After what feels like an eternity, my door opens. Branson takes my hand and guides me out of the car and into the house. The front door closes behind us; he pushes me to the wall and slams his lips on mine. My arms wrap around his shoulders and I pull him to me. He slides his hand down my body, inching under my dress and up my thigh. He rubs me through my panties and I moan into this kiss.

"Please, Branson," I murmur against his lips.

He pulls my panties to the side, I'm soaked and he easily slips his finger inside me. Again, I moan. He wriggles his finger around and adds a second digit. Out of nowhere, my orgasm explodes; my legs become jelly as the pleasure resonates throughout my body. "That's one," he whispers in my ear.

Placing his hands under my ass, he lifts me up. I wrap my legs around his waist and shamelessly rub myself on his erection, his rock-hard erection. He starts moving and I think he's going into our room, but he stops and places me on my feet. He spins me around and whispers, "Hands on the counter." I can hear his fly lower and my tummy clenches, I know what's coming next. He kicks my feet apart, and just like we always do in this spot, he lifts my dress over my hips, pulls my panties down, and slams himself inside me from behind. He grips my hips and begins to piston his hips. Sliding my hand down, I rub my clit in circles. His thrusts become more hurried and he growls, "Now." And together we tumble over into the abyss, moaning each other's names as we come.

Pulling me up, he wraps his arms around me, cupping my breasts, and huskily says, "That's two."

Laughing, I turn my head over my shoulder; he leans forward and kisses me. "I love you, Branson Holmes."

"I love you too, Kasey Wellson, soon-to-be Holmes."

Spinning around to face him, I lift my hands and remove the blindfold, dropping it on the counter beside us. When my vision clears and he comes into focus again, I smile.

"Hi."

"Hi," he murmurs back.

We stare at each other. No words are spoken but at the same time, all the words are articulated.

He lifts me up so I'm perched on the edge of the counter, he leans behind me and slides a wine bucket over and pours us each a glass of white wine. He hands me a glass and picks up his. "Happy Valentine's Day."

"Happy Valentine's Day."

We clink our glasses together and drink. Our eyes locked on one another, the air around us thickens with desire and lust. My heart rate accelerates, excited to see what happens next...and I don't have to wait long to find out.

Branson pushes me back so I'm lying on the countertop. He grabs a piece of ice out of the bucket and run it up my thigh, pushing my dress up as he goes. He circles the cube over my clit, and I squirm at the coldness, but then it's warm as he sucks and nibbles my clit.

Running my fingers through his hair, I grip his head and push him farther into me. Taking the hint, he attacks my pussy. We haven't had sex since Kody was born, and I'm on the cusp of orgasm number three. It sneaks up on me and when Branson thrusts his finger into me, I explode. Soaking his face and hands.

Standing up, he smirks. "That's three." I pant. We both laugh.

The rest of the night proceeds in a very sexy way. We eat. We have sex. We make out. We fall deeper and deeper in love. It's the perfect Valentine's Day, and the perfect reintroduction into our sex life together. Sex with Branson while pregnant was awesome —thank you, hormones—but sex with him not pregnant, is out of this world amazing. I'm one lucky lady...

Walking into the kitchen, I stare at the counter and smile. Leaning on the granite in 'our' spot, I watch everyone. All those who are near and dear to us are here to celebrate KJ's birthday. I do wish Kody was here to see his son grow, but I know that he's watching over us.

The last two years have flown by, and at times, they were rough, really rough. There have been ups and there have been downs, but I managed to survive. And I only did that because of our friends and family, but mostly it was KJ and Branson who got me though it all, they are my everything. I would not have survived without them.

The first anniversary of Kody's passing was tough, really tough. The three of us went to the cemetery and visited. It was a sad day, but it was also the day KJ sat up unassisted for the first time. After that, there was no stopping our little terror...who still thinks nighttime equals party time, but thankfully, we are getting a few nights here and there where he sleeps through.

In August, Stacey and my friends flew me back to Kansas and I finally got my lap dance from Jake, and let me tell you, it was worth the wait. Holy abs, Batman, that man sure knows how to swivel his hips. The following weekend, I married Branson in an intimate ceremony at Bin 501, followed by a wild reception where copious bottles of wine were drunk but most of all, I got to marry my Prince Charming.

Now we are in December, celebrating KJ's first birthday. I can quite easily say that December is my favorite time of year. It's the month KJ was born; the month Branson and I got engaged, AND it's the month I found out I was expecting baby number two...and three.

EXTENDED EPILOGUE
KASEY

...May 4th, 2028

OPENING THE DOOR, I SMILE AT MARLEE AND SEE A NOT-SO-little-anymore blonde tuft of hair fly past me. Amelia races inside, shouting to KJ, Gracie, and Ginny that she has arrived...just like she does every time Marlee and Gage pop over.

"Hey, Marlee, how you doing?"

"Good. Thank you so much for watching Amelia tonight, we really appreciate it."

"Happy to do it, she's an angel PLUS everyone needs a special night out every now and then." I wink at her as I say this, Marlee's cheeks tinge pink with embarrassment and I giggle on the inside at her reaction.

"That is true, but I feel like you guys watch her all the time and I never do anything to help you and Branson out. You have three kids, we only have one."

"You do plenty for us, besides, it will get the kids used to having someone else around," I say, as I rest my palm on my lower back and push out my tummy, showing off my slight baby bump.

Her eyes pop open at my statement. "You're pregnant again?"

Nodding my head up and down, I purse my lips and then laugh. "Yep, my ever virile husband knocked me up just before he had his vasectomy."

A laugh escapes Marlee's lips and she tries hard not to grin, she fails miserably at this. "Ohh my God, Kase, that's way too funny. Looks like his super sperm wanted one last shot before they died a grizzly, snippy death." She laughs at her own joke and then her face turns serious and she quietly asks, "Are we excited about this baby surprise?"

Nodding my head yes again, I flash a joyous smile. "Yeah, we are excited to be expanding our family. Sure, it was a surprise—a hell of a surprise—but yeah; we are super excited. So are the kids." As I say this, Branson steps behind me and cups my tummy, kissing the side of my head. I lean back into him and smile. I love being in his arms like this.

"Pretty awesome news, hey?" He beams.

"What's awesome news?" Gage asks, as he steps outside after dropping off Amelia's things. He pulls Marlee into his arms, mirroring my and Branson's embrace.

"They're having another baby," Marlee tells him.

"Didn't you just have the snip?" He mimics the scissor motion with his fingers.

"It happened the week before I had the procedure."

"No shit," Gage scoffs. "Way to go, you and your super human sperm." Gage and Branson fist bump, then he kisses me on the cheek. "Congrats, Buttercup." I scowl at him, and then he scrunches his face up. "Does that mean you will be chowing down on snow peas and salsa again?"

"Considering with Gracie and Ginny I craved licorice, anything is possible." Just to tease him, I cheekily add, "Maybe this time it will be licorice and salsa."

"Ugh, that's just nasty, why are you so mean to me?" I shrug my shoulders at him and grin. "And on that note," he says, "I'm going to whisk my wife away for a romantic evening, just the two of us."

"Have fun, you two," I say and watch them walk toward their sedan. My eyes well with tears; damn pregnancy hormones. I'm happy Gage got his happily ever after, and Marlee is just perfect for him.

The night with Amelia was fun, just like it always is. She really is a gorgeous girl, and it makes me hope this little one is a girl again, but I would also like it to be a boy. I'd love for Branson to have a biological son of his own.

Looking out to the backyard, I watch Branson goof around with the four kids and find myself grinning, just as a wave of morning sickness hits. Racing into the bathroom, I make it to the toilet just in time to empty my stomach.

This pregnancy is the hardest so far, the morning sickness is horrendous and I'm constantly exhausted from throwing up all the time. With KJ and the twins, I had the odd day here and there, but with this lil' Minion, it's every day…several times every day.

Branson walks in and hands me a glass of water. "You okay, baby?"

"Ugh, I'm dying. I kinda hate you right now. Why couldn't your super sperm not be so super. Or like wait a week to die with the other sperms after your snip?"

He shrugs at me. "Are you sure you want to go this afternoon?"

"Yeah, I'm sure." I take a sip of my water. "Besides, I think KJ needs it. He seems off at the moment."

"You noticed too, huh?"

Standing up, I nod. "Yeah, I have. Do you think this pregnancy has anything to do with it? He was too little when we had the girls, but now he's older; he's aware and thinking about it. I think he feels like he's going to be left out since you will have three biological kids."

"I think you might be right, Kase. How about we drop Amelia home and spend the whole afternoon with Kody? I think KJ will like that."

"Sounds like a plan. Give me a sec to freshen up."

"Will do. I'll wrangle the kids and you look after you and our lil' Minion."

He steps toward me and places a kiss on my lips; I push him back. "Eeeeew, I have vomit breath."

"I love you, even with vomit breath."

"That's so gross, Branson." I push him on the chest. "Go, we can kiss once I have minty fresh breath again."

"Promise?"

"Promise."

He winks at me and exits the bathroom, leaving me to freshen up. As I brush my teeth, my mind drifts to the night Minion was conceived...

• • •

…*The kids are all tucked into bed and sound asleep. Branson and I are sitting out on the patio, snuggling on the daybed, watching the flames of the firepit flicker and crackle. The evening is warm but the slight breeze makes it perfect. It's probably a little hot for a fire, but nothing beats the ambiance of a fire.*

Branson tops off my wine glass, hands it back to me, and kisses the side of my head and whispers, "I love you, Kasey," as he snuggles beside me.

"I love you too." Looking up at him, my insides quiver at how sexy he looks right in this moment. Taking his wine glass from him, I place them both on the ground. Turning to him, I straddle his hips, my skirt bunching around my waist. I lower my mouth to his and kiss him. His hands palm my ass and I grind myself on his pelvis as the intensity of our kiss increases. Sliding my hands into his hair, I run my fingers across his scalp, and back around to cup his cheeks in my hands.

Breaking the connection, I pull back. His eyes are full of hunger and carnal desire, just like mine. "Make love to me," I whisper, as I reach down and lift my sweater over my head, dropping it to the ground. Reaching behind me, I unclasp my bra, he immediately leans forward and takes a nipple into his mouth. Gently biting down on the taut peak before sucking. "Branson," I moan, as my head drops back and I give myself over to the pleasure coursing through my body.

He pulls his Henley over his head, dropping it to the floor, knocking the wine glasses over but neither of us care. He presses his lips to mine again, his arms tightening around my shoulders. He flips me onto my back. Hovering above me, he cocoons me underneath him, his lips never leaving mine as he does this.

Raking my hands down his back, I squeeze his ass through his jeans. Sliding my hands around his hips, I quickly make work of his zipper and fly before pushing the material down. Using my feet, I slide them the rest of the way off.

He runs his hand up my thigh, cupping my mound over the top of my panties. Pressing his thumb against my clit, I buck at the sensation. "Please, Branson," I whisper, as I lift myself up and press my lips to his. Grinding myself on his hand, he pushes my panties aside and presses two fingers inside me. I moan at the sensation as he starts to plunge them in and out of my slick folds.

We kiss, our tongues caressing one another. My orgasm builds, he pinches my nipple with his other hand and I explode all over this fingers.

He pulls them out and looks down at me, he slips them into his mouth and sucks them clean. While he licks his fingers, I shimmy my skirt and panties down my legs, lying before him naked and ready for him to devour me. The reflection of the flames from the fire flicker across my skin.

"You are the sexiest woman alive," Branson declares, as he stares down at me. His eyes are locked on mine as he slides himself inside. We both moan as my walls clench around him. With our eyes locked on one another, we make love under the stars. Each reaching our peak at the same time. Moaning each other's name as we let our orgasms roar through our bodies.

Lying down next to me, I roll onto my side and snuggle into him. Resting my head on his chest, I close my eyes and drift off to sleep. Only to be woken up when Branson lifts me into his arms, bridal style, and walks us inside. Placing me on the bed, we make love again before blissfully falling asleep wrapped in each other's embrace...

I'm snapped back to the present as another wave of morning sickness hits. I throw up another three times before we leave.

EXTENDED EPILOGUE
BRANSON

Like always when we come to visit Kody, I head over first and have a chat with my brother. All these years later, it still hurts that he's gone. I miss him each and every single day. He's already missed out on so much; seeing KJ grow up, and more to come like graduation, and getting married. Seeing Bin 501 thrive. He's missing it all. That hurts just as much as losing him does. But what I'm most sad about is I lost my best friend when he died. We were more than just brothers, he was my other half. That was until Kasey found two unexpected letters that changed everything.

Staring at Kody's headstone, I sigh and take a seat, leaning against the granite. "Bro, I wish you were here. I still miss you today just as much as I did when we first lost you." Looking up, I see Kase, KJ, Gracie ,and Ginny walking toward us. "Dude, you'd be so proud of KJ and Kase. Your son is so much like you, and when he smiles, it's like I'm staring at you when we were little. He's a mini-you in so many ways. Kase and I talk about you with him all the time. And your nieces are little firecrackers, just like their mom." *I wonder what this next one will be like?* "Ohh yeah, we are pregnant again. I knocked Kasey up the week before my snip." I laugh at that, and I'm positive I will for the rest of my life.

I watch as the three, well four, most important people in my life walk toward me and a wave of guilt crashes over me at my happiness. I feel guilty for what I now have. If Kody were still alive, I wouldn't have a sexy as sin wife, or two gorgeous daughters who are mini versions of their mother, or another on the way. Sure, I'd have my brother but I'd be missing out on so much more. Does that make me a horrible person? How can I be happy yet also devastated that someone is gone?

"Daddy," Gracie says as she jumps into my lap.

"Hey, Pumpkin." I place a kiss on her temple and breath in her strawberry shampoo.

She climbs off my lap and hugs Kody's headstone, "Hi, Uncle Kody. Ginny and I are going to be big sisters, how cool is that?"

KJ rolls his eyes at Gracie, the attitude is starting to creep in with him. He's like the perfect mixture of Kody and me, add in Kasey's sass, and we are totally screwed when he hits his teens He stares at the headstone and then sadly smiles at me. "Hey, Dad."

"Hey, Buddy. You okay?"

"Yeah, I just hate that I never got to know Pops. I know you and Mom have told me countless stories. As have

Nana and Pop Pop, but I still feel like a part of me is missing." He pauses and swallows. "And, Dad, I feel like a dick," I eye him at his language but he shrugs, "saying that, 'cause I don't want to hurt you, but I hate that I didn't get to meet him or know him. I wonder every day if I'm making him proud."

"KJ," I say, as I stand up and squeeze his shoulder. "You don't ever apologize for how you feel, not when it comes to Kody. Our story sucks ass, but I promise you one thing, your dad would be so proud of the person you are. You may only be eight, almost nine, but you are wise beyond your years, just like he was. You are so much like him, KJ, so much. I guarantee you, he'll be up there," I point to the heavens, "watching over you with a grin on his face and joy in his heart."

"You think?"

I nod my head. "I know so, and you know why I know so?"

"Why?"

"Because I'm proud of you."

"You are?" His eyes light up at my statement.

Again, I nod my head, "Very much so. I'll let you in on a secret. I love and miss your dad just as much as anyone else in our family. It sucks that he died, but the one good thing from that; I get to call you my son. KJ, I love you as if you were my own. "

He wipes at his eyes. "I love you too, Dad." He wraps his arms around my waist and rests his head on my stomach. Wrapping my arms around him, I hug him back. Bending down, I place a kiss on his head and close my eyes, as I hug my son. And he is my son, in every aspect of the word.

When I look up again, I see Kasey staring at us, tears in

her eyes. She walks toward us, and without a word, she wraps her arms around KJ and me, sandwiching him between us.

"Mom," KJ whines, "you're squishing me."

"Shhhh, I'm hugging my boys," she whispers as tears stream down her face.

Kissing her temple, she lifts her gaze to mine. "I love you, Branson Holmes."

"I love you, Kasey Holmes."

She lifts up on her toes and kisses my lips. The moment is broken when KJ pushes on me. "Eeeeew, don't do that with me here." He slips out from between us and takes a seat next to Kody's headstone. Gracie jumps into his lap, Ginny pushes her way in and leans toward the headstone and whispers, "Hey, Uncle K. Mom and Dad are smooching again and that's so gross. I'm never going to smooch a boy like that."

Kasey and I laugh at our little drama queen. With her arms still around my waist, she looks up at me. "You guys okay?"

"Yeah. Just a father/son moment."

"Ohh, Branson," she cries, "You really are amazing. You are my rock. You were his rock when he as alive. You are everyone's rock. You are so strong and I'm so happy with you, but at the same time, I feel like a bitch saying that because someone died. Someone I loved with all my heart. Someone I still love dearly." She swallows back a sob, "Will the guilt at loving you ever go away?"

"I don't know but know that I feel the same. I loved my brother with everything, but if he were still alive, I wouldn't have you, Gracie, or Ginny. I'd know KJ in a completely different way and this lil' Minion wouldn't exist." I lower my hands to her belly. "Our situation is unique, so fucking unique, but it was if Kody knew this would happen. His letters to each of us prove that."

"You know, without that letter, I never would have acted on my feelings. It was so unexpected to find them, but at the same time not, because Kody was a planner like that. I mean, look at his funeral? I didn't have to do a thing because it was all sorted. Thank God for that cause I was a wreck."

"Wreck was an understatement," I joke.

She smacks me in the stomach. "Hey, there were other circumstances that added to my emotions."

"That is true and he's growing into a fine young man. I know Kody would be proud."

"So proud," Kasey reiterates my statement and wipes at her eye.

"Mommy, come talk to Uncle Kody?" Gracie asks.

Kasey steps away from me and over to the kids. She takes a seat and Gracie climbs off KJ's lap and into hers. I stand back and watch as they all talk and laugh. Looking to the sky, I whisper, "I promise to look after them for you, Bro, just like your letter asked."

Walking over to my family, I take a seat behind Kasey. She snuggles into me and the five of us chat to Kody about the latest developments in the Holmes household, and what we have been up to since our last visit. KJ seems more at ease and his eyes reflect that joy.

Watching my family, I smile. I really am a lucky man because those two unexpected letters from my brother gave me all of this.

THE END!!!!!

Read on for a sneak peek at The Unexpected Package.

CHAPTER 1
…12th December 2019

"Sign here please." The young delivery guy's voice breaking the silence in reception. His tone arrogant and the sassitude from his is on fire. He drops the clipboard onto my desk and stares at me in a 'hurry up, I got other shit to do' kind of way.

Shaking my head at the lil' punks rudeness, I look down at the board but I don't see WFOX-FM listed, "Ummm, where did you need me to sign?"

"Line three." He huffs and rolls his eyes. *Asshole.*

Looking to line three I notice that it's not for us, "You are on the wrong floor, you want BKB Inc—"

"Don't care, just sign or I return it to the depot as undeliverable."

Shaking my head and rolling my eyes, I pick up my pen and scribble my signature; I normally wouldn't sign for something that isn't mine but for some reason, I feel like I *need* to sign for this package. He dumps a box on my desk, picks up his clipboard and turns to leave. The elevator doors open, and he shoves aside Kasey as she steps out.

"Watch where you're going fatty." He snarls.

"Excuse me, what did you say you little shithead?" Kasey snaps back but the elevator doors close before she gets a reply.

"What a little asshole." Kasey mumbles to herself as she waddles over to me. "Hey, Stace."

"Asshole alright. The shithead, made me sign for this." Pointing to the box. "It's for the next floor up."

"Why?" Kasey asks, rubbing her lower back.

"Cause as you stated, he's an asshole shithead douche-hole. You okay?"

"Yeah, my lower back is killing me. I'm so over being pregnant." But I know she's lying, the smile on her face tells me otherwise, and if anyone deserves to be happy it's her. This year has been tough for Kase but she's come out on top and I've never seen her looking happier than she is now. I feel like a bitch thinking that because she was happy with Kody but with Branson, it's another level of happy. It's like she found that missing piece and now, she's on cloud nine million.

"I can't believe you are still working. You should be on maternity leave already. Sitting on the couch, eating that horrible stuff you can't get enough of and watching Days of our Lives."

"Don't start, you sound like Branson, and it's the best food ever. Pretty sure I'll be fine, tomorrow is my last day and come next week I'll be doing exactly what you said. But instead of that crap you watch, I'll be drooling over Sam and Dean."

"Supernatural, nice. I'll allow that amendment."

"Thanks."

"Any chance you'll amend the shit you eat?"

"Nope, that 'shit' as you so call it is divine."

"Yeah, nah, not divine at all, Kase. With you gone, so will that nasty snow pea and salsa shit."

"You know, it feels like everyone is trying to get rid of me."

"Why would we want to do that Buttercup?" Gage says as he drops some envelopes in the outgoing mail pile.

A laugh escapes when I hear him call her Buttercup. "Dude, don't engage her," I say, as I notice Kase poke her tongue at our marketing manager, "she's hangry and the delivery ass just insulted her."

"I'll risk it, I have to get it in the jabs while I can." He nonchalantly says, he turns to Kase and places his arm around her shoulder, "This place won't be the same when you go on mat leave."

"Pffft," she scoffs, "You won't miss me at all."

"We won't miss your snow pea and salsa obsession." Stacey says, "That shit is nasty."

"Is not." She scoffs in reply.

"Great comeback there, Buttercup, but Stace is right, that shit is nasty as fuck." Gage shudders as he says this.

Kasey pushes him away, "Fuck off asshole." she scoffs. Flipping him the bird as she waddles down the hall towards her office.

Gage and I both laugh.

Standing up, I grab the mystery package and place it on my desk when I notice Gage lingering. "You all good?"

"Yeah, just realizing that I really will miss her when she goes on maternity leave."

"Place definitely won't be the same without her." I sigh, "Do you think she'll be okay?"

"Yeah." He nods, "She has Branson."

"He does love her unconditionally." I say, wishing that I had someone love me like Branson loves her. Sure, their relationship is a tad unconventional, considering he's her dead baby daddy's brother but Kody, rest his soul, must have known something was going to happen to him because from beyond the grave, he gave his blessing.

"You'll find someone." Gage says, bringing me back to the present.

"Huh?" I deadpan, confused at his statement.

"You'll find your one. Kasey found hers, twice and I found mine. If a grinch like me can, you will too."

"You've become Mr. Philosophical, when it comes to love and shit. How do you do that? How do you know what I'm thinking?"

"Marlee. She brings out the best in me." And with that statement, he turns and heads back to his office and as I watch him walk away from me, I wonder if he's right. Will I ever find my one true love? My track record with men hasn't been the best. There was Jon, the unemployed accountant. Then there was Evan, the two timing pin-dick. And the latest loser in the Stacey Thomms dating disaster folio was Gavin the attorney; I really thought he was the one…but then he was arrested for withholding evidence and money laundering. Clearly I have great taste in men— not—maybe I should become a lesbian. Chicks are easier to manage and decipher, Nah I love dick too much so that's a firm no on becoming a lesbian. Maybe I'm destined to be alone due to something terrible that I did in a past life. Shaking my head, I grab the delivery, and head up to BKB Incorporated to deliver their package.

Little did I know, this unexpected package was about to change my life.

The Unexpected Package is out now.

ACKNOWLEDGMENTS

Chloe Renee', thank you for letting June aka Jake appear in my story. That scene really set the book and I could not have done it without you. Your support and encouragement means everything to me, thank you doesn't cut it but it's all I've got for now.

To my husband, **Troy** and my munchkins, **Piper** and **Kade**; you three are my biggest supporters and I love you all dearly.

My beta babes, **Halle, Crissy, Amanda** and **Shez**; I would be lost without you ladies. Thank you for your feedback, support, guidance and encouragement. Love you gals to the moon and back.

My editor, **Karen** from **Barren Acres Editing**; thank you for everything. You push me to be the best author *THAT* I can be. I value your friendship, feedback, skills and support. I look forward to the day that we finally meet.

My cover designer, **Dana Leah** from **Designs by Dana;** thank you for turning an already stunning cover into another stunning design. I loved the December cover and I still love this one now. Thank you again for the amendment and beautiful covers.

And finally, **you, my readers;** this is book number ten and I would not be here without you and your support. Thank you for coming along on this journey with me; I appreciate each and every single one of you. Your messages and reviews mean everything to me and I will be forever grateful to you all XoXoX

ALSO BY DL GALLIE

THE CASTAWAY GROVE COLLECTION

Love has arrived in the Grove

Oasis

Unequivocal Love

Five Words

Broken Rules - coming mid/late 2020

…and a few more as well.

THE LIQUOR CABINET SERIES

Liquor has never been so disturbingly saucy

Malt Me (Book 1)

Tequila Healing (Book 2)

Wine Not (Book 3)

The Final Shot (Book 4)

The Liquor Cabinet: Series boxset

THE UNEXPECTED SERIES

When it comes to love, expect the unexpected

The Unexpected Gift

The Unexpected Letter

The Unexpected Package

The Unexpected Connection

STAND ALONES

Out of Nowhere

Antecedent

Seven Nights

Falling for Dr. Kelly, a Falling novel

Falling for Dr. Knight, a Falling novel - coming May 2020

Doc Steel - coming June 2020

The Dirty Dozen: Alpha edition

The Rule Breaker Anthology - coming soon

In the Dark of Night anthology (only available in paperback directly from me)

Titanic Tales, a charity anthology (no longer available)

Gone Coastal, a sizzling summer beach anthology (no longer available)

Leave Me Breathless: The Lilac Collection (no longer available)

ABOUT THE AUTHOR

DL Gallie is from Queensland, Australia, but she's lived in many different places all over the world, including the UK and Canada. She currently resides in Central Queensland with her husband and two munchkins. She and her husband have been together  since she was sixteen, and although they drive each other crazy at times, she couldn't imagine her life without him.

Shortly after her son was born, DL began reading again. With encouragement from her husband, she picked up the pen and started writing, and now the voices in her head won't shut up.

DL enjoys listening to music, drinking white wine in the summer, red wine in the winter, and beer all year round. She's also never been known to turn down a cocktail, especially a margarita.